"Yes'm"

"Yes 'm"

J. M. Duke

iUniverse, Inc.
Bloomington

"Yes'm"

Copyright © 2012 by J. M. Duke.

All rights reserved. No part of this book may be used or reproduced by any means, graphic, electronic, or mechanical, including photocopying, recording, taping or by any information storage retrieval system without the written permission of the publisher except in the case of brief quotations embodied in critical articles and reviews.

This is a work of fiction. Names, characters, places, and incidents either are the product of the author's imagination or are used fictitiously, and any resemblance to actual persons, living or dead, business establishments, events, or locales is entirely coincidental. The publisher does not have any control over and does not assume responsibility for third-party websites or their content.

iUniverse books may be ordered through booksellers or by contacting:

iUniverse
1663 Liberty Drive
Bloomington, IN 47403
www.iuniverse.com
1-800-Authors (1-800-288-4677)

Because of the dynamic nature of the Internet, any web addresses or links contained in this book may have changed since publication and may no longer be valid. The views expressed in this work are solely those of the author and do not necessarily reflect the views of the publisher, and the publisher hereby disclaims any responsibility for them.

Any people depicted in stock imagery provided by Thinkstock are models, and such images are being used for illustrative purposes only.
Certain stock imagery © Thinkstock.

ISBN: 978-1-4759-5581-1 (sc)
ISBN: 978-1-4759-5580-4 (hc)
ISBN: 978-1-4759-5579-8 (ebk)

Library of Congress Control Number: 2012919738

Printed in the United States of America

iUniverse rev. date: 10/20/2012

*In memory of the many good times
I shared among a loving family,
in a wonderful town,
Surrounded by the very best
friends and neighbors.*

Introduction

I open my eyes from a good night's sleep to find the sun streaming in through the sheer panels that cover the window. An early morning ocean breeze floats across my bed. I can hear the waves as they break against our dock and are occasionally interrupted by the low groan of a taut rope struggling to secure our jet ski. What an exquisite morning, I think. I'll just lie back for another minute or two to take it in. *Ahhhh*, life is good. I stretch my arms out over my head and draw in a deep calming breath. "Damn!" I rise up quickly, "Its cold in here!" I throw back the summer cover, remind myself to find the comforter, and rush across the room to close the window. Along the way, body ahead of brain, I catch my pajamas on the rocking chair and lose my balance. "Shit!" I mumble. I have stubbed my little toe and immediately draw into a standing fetal position., beloved toe in hand. "Man," I whisper, hopping on one leg to the bed. It seems the older I get the more often I hold these private two-way conversations so I whisper. My husband is becoming slightly concerned. "Hey," I proclaim quietly, "I am standing on one leg! That is pretty impressive. You go, old girl," and reach back to give myself a little atta' boy. Now resting safely on the edge of the bed I bend forward to inspect my toe. "Oh, I need my glasses," and reach over to retrieve them from the nightstand. Wiggle, wiggle, yes, it bends, it's all right, and return my foot to the floor. Perched for a moment in utter silence, I let out a quiet *snort* of self-amusement: The story of my life.

Uh, oh, he's heard me moving. Not my husband, the dog. "Good morning, Toby. Yes, good morning, you good boy. What you want?

You ready for a walk on the beach?" I find it amusing that somehow it's socially acceptable to hold a conversation with a dog, but not one's self. I shrug; it is beyond me. Toby bounces around the room like "Tigger." I am forced to dodge my slippers, shoes and dust balls, as they are hurled and now airborne. "Toby," I command, using my alpha dog tone, "Stop." He freezes in place, almost, drool is involuntarily hanging from the sides of his mouth, and his massive tail is in constant motion, seemingly with a mind of its own. I hear my watch hit the floor as it is swept from the nightstand. I'll get it later, I think; if I can remember where it is. I stand and throw on a pair of old blue jeans, reach for my oversized gray sweatshirt, no bra (hippie that I was), pull back my long, now a mix of auburn and gray, hair. Voila', I'm ready to face the day. I give the mirror a glimpse; not too bad, I think, considering, and turn. "Toby, come."

"Morning, hon," I yell through the walls to my hard-working husband. He's younger than I, but thinks as if he were older, the responsible one, if you get my drift. Yes, he's a serious one. "God gives you what you need," I can hear Pearl's words inside my head, and inadvertently nod. He has provided our family with a good stable life: our children and grandchildren with security. I tend to be more of a "free spirit." Always have. I take great pride in my elusive and relaxed persona. I would like to think that material things in my life don't matter, but hell, that wouldn't be true. I am, however, the one, who, as the world falls around us, will throw out a bit of sarcasm to lighten the mood, you know, reassuringly. "Well," I might say, "It could be worse. At least if the bank takes your home, you'll always have your dimples." Seriously, I love sarcasm. I was raised with sarcasm. From my viewpoint, a good sarcastic wit is a measure of one's intelligence. My brother and I used to go back and forth for hours matching wits, but Mom, now she was the champion. "Don't want to go there," I remind myself, quietly and out loud. I shrug my shoulders.

I drag myself into the kitchen, to find my husband sitting staunchly at the table, drinking his morning coffee and reading the newspaper on his computer; all parts of his daily ritual. He likes organization, schedules and rituals. I soon find myself humming in jest, "May the circle, be unbroken . . ." oops. I *snort* again. "Morning," he says, looking up, all bright-eyed and bushy—tailed, in his perfect suit, with the perfect hair and the perfect disposition. "Really," he asks, "With all the money I spend on your clothes that's all you can find to wear?" I laugh; he has a point, but I hold my hands out to my sides and sing, "I'm too sexy for my shirt . . . too sexy for my shirt," rotating around in circles. He just shakes his head and walks over to kiss me good-bye. Just like love, he is patient and kind.

I turn to open the door and think, gosh, I do love retirement. "Come on, boy. Let's go." On my way outside, I reach over the old wooden rail to grab my old rusty aluminum chair, the one with the sagging seat that fits my old behind perfectly. I swerve to avoid Toby as he stops to lift his leg on the flagpole. "Toby, show some respect!" I say, "Your Daddy's a veteran. Geez." His eyes acknowledge my existence, but the flow continues uninterrupted. Together we walk toward the beach. This is our favorite place in the world. It's quiet, with very little human contact. Which brings up another "bone of contention," my husband complains that I am not social. "You need to make friends!" he says, like a Jewish mother, no insult intended, all aglow with concern, "It would be good for you," he over-analyzes.

"Yes, Dr. Phil," I say, holding his glare. "Look, honey," I try to explain. "I am a family person. My family is nearly gone. I spend time with the kids and grandkids, and that's all I want. As for friends, I have a lot of friends. I like old friends, tried and true. They are spread all over the country, so we *Facebook*. You do know what *Facebook* is? Right?" I ask, oozing sarcasm. He tilts his head. He's quick. "But honestly," I continue, "I'm good. By the time I get to know someone new, they'll probably move or die anyway. So what's the point? Now, if you mean, make acquaintances, I have. I always make sure to stop and speak politely to the Wal-Mart clerk, every time I'm in there." *Snort.* He gives me his condescending eye-roll. I counter with a patronizing eye-roll, and say, "Honey, don't start. I really do love you, but go on to work, huh? I'm fine." His face drops, lips in a pout, rejected. He's also very sensitive. "Oh, God," I pronounce, throwing my body into a spin. For some reason, emotional people completely stress me out. The maintenance they require literally "sucks the life" out of me. I mean, what can I do? Several times a year I propose to weigh my words more carefully, before they spew out of my mouth like a leaky pipe, but that just makes it too difficult to talk, so I give up in defeat. "Bye, honey. Have a good day," I say, my eyelashes a flutter, air kiss, air kiss. My husband is a people person. Me, not so much, each of these conversations always leaves me longing for my brother. He'd understand.

"My people," as people say, are mostly gone now. I miss them, tons. I miss their wit and their quirks and their rudeness and their love. I miss their love, good, bad or indifferent. I miss it. I love to sit on the beach, watch the dog run and remember the "the good ole' days" occasionally interrupted by a "not so good ole' day." Of course, it makes me a little sad, but I am grateful to have shared my life with theirs. "All good things must come to an end," I hear Pearl again, "Just how it is."

I am all of five feet, 125 pounds, passive/non-aggressive, well usually, unless provoked. I am one tough cookie. There really isn't too much that bothers me. Well, unless you mess with one of my kids. Then I'll swell up right before your eyes to six feet and bullet proof. "Sam," I whisper to myself, "You have become one foolish old woman." Yes, well, I whisper, I'm am 61—62 next month—and easily humored.

"Toby," I yell, "Get!" I swat him away because whenever he is soaking wet and full of sand he must walk all the way back to me to shake. Now my clean sweatshirt is spattered with sand. Good thing I have some others, I think, recognizing my good fortune. Now where is that freaking chair? Oh, next to me. I haven't moved just been standing in place, so I reach down to get it. As I walk along I struggle to open the folded chair into position. Gosh, I think, what's it take to open this contraption, an engineer? I approach the ocean searching for just the right place. I need to be selective because I may still be sitting here when the tide comes in; and suppose I fall asleep. "Only thing I mind is if the tide's going to reach my chair," I sing, and jig a little, before sitting down.

"*Ahhhh*," I whisper. Flash! A thought runs across my mind. My retirement party, "Oh," my colleagues said, "You will be so bored."

"Not!" I yell, from my chair, looking back to make sure that my husband's car is gone. Well, I admit, old age, by itself isn't so good, but I'm holding up reasonably well, so far. I settle back and prepare to hear my own thoughts for the rest of the day, hopefully, without interruption. The memories replay through my mind like an old movie reel as I ponder, just how exactly did I arrive at this point: An old activist, all worn out from activity. Sarcastic. Slightly eccentric, maybe. Occasionally offensive. And just a tad unpredictable. Worse, I'm completely okay with it. In fact, I love the person I've become.

I lean my head back against the chair, and roll my eyes around to look for Toby. He is sleeping by my side. I close my eyes, and whisper,

> "Carry me back to old Virginny.
>
> There's where we'll meet and we'll never part no more."

SMALL TOWN, VIRGINIA, 1950

Chapter One

It's an unusually cold and blustery November day in Virginia. A recent snow lightly covers the ground. A southern gentleman clad in his hat and heavy overcoat steadies his way along a slippery sidewalk while supporting the elbow of his pregnant wife. Their immediate destination is a pre-warmed 1947 Plymouth, waiting in front of their house.

Most of the neighbors whose homes line the street step out onto their front stoop to send good wishes and support to the expectant couple. As is common for the time, the neighbors will not retreat to the warmth of their home until the car is no longer in sight.

Perched on the front porch of the couple's home, supervising a safe transition to the car, and undaunted by the cold weather, is Pearl, the family caretaker. Pearl doesn't usually spend the night at her employer's home, but tonight is an exception. She has arrived to care for the couple's older son while the Mister and Missus tend to the business at hand. Her light cotton dress blows in the wind to expose her knee-high stockings, while her right arm is wrapped securely around the shoulder of the little boy leaning against her hip.

As the young mother reaches the security of the vehicle, she turns to look back at her son. He lifts his shirtsleeve to his face to wipe away his tears. The heavy car doors slam shut and a moment later the tires find traction in the gravel and pull forward. The people along the street all raise their hands to bid them safe travel. The street is silent, but for the sound of the distant car tires against the snow.

The nearest hospital is located in the next county, a one and one-half hour trip in good weather. The town does have three local doctors, all general practitioners, who do not encourage home birth or midwives unless absolutely unavoidable. Doctors are indeed the backbone and saviors of this community, particularly when it comes to the repair of broken limbs, the administration of a needed tetanus shot or a prescription for the often needed antibiotic. But the doctors are cautious and admittedly ill-equipped for a complication associated with childbirth.

The old Plymouth makes its way along 25 miles of snow and gravel-covered two lane country roads. The driver will occasionally have to pull the car dangerously close to the ditch so an approaching vehicle can pass. Time, however, is not of the essence, as this particular labor is to be induced. The labor will later be described as a most horrific, terrifying and unforgettable experience for the young expectant mother and her anxious and apprehensive husband.

Arriving at the hospital, the husband parks in front of the entrance, circles around the car to offer a firm hand of support to his wife. With her feet securely on the ground, he wraps his arms around her, pulling her close. "I love you," he whispers. "Don't worry," she says, bending back to look into his eyes, "We will be all right."

Greeting them inside the door is a ramrod straight, oversized nurse. "Please follow me," she directs the mother. The gentleman takes a small step back, releasing the hand of his wife. She leans in to give him a reassuring peck on the mouth before she leaves. He will not move until she is no longer in sight.

Midway down a long white corridor, the soon-to-be mother is directed through a doorway into an impersonally and equally cold white room. The walls are lined with beds, each separated by white curtains. She hesitates when she hears an orchestra of grunts and groans. "This way," the nurse encourages, "It will be fine. We do this all the time."

Back In the waiting room, sleep escapes the expectant father. He now lies on a cot he has fashioned from a row of hard plastic chairs. Hours later, he hears the distinct sound of footsteps padding down the hallway. He sits up, anxious to hear the news.

"Sir," the doctor says, holding out a congratulatory hand, "You are the father of a healthy little girl! Mother and daughter are both doing well. She arrived to the world kicking and screaming, but she is strong and healthy. We will need to keep your wife and the baby in the hospital for about a week. That's just standard hospital procedure. Right now you may go visit your wife and greet your daughter. Then, I suggest, you make your way home to rest while you can."

"Samantha Lee," the father whispers, "my little girl. How your Daddy loves you."

Chapter Two

Hi. My name is Sam. My given name is Samantha Lee. I was named after one of my grandfathers.

My family, like most, includes grandparents, uncles, aunts, cousins, and a brother. I liken the group to that of a "clan." Not the "k" type Klan, but the "c" type clan, defined as a group of closely-knit and interrelated families, like the Kennedys, but more along the lines of the Hatfields or McCoys. The fact is, we can usually be found together, occasionally broken out into smaller groups, but rarely alone.

We hail from the Shenandoah Valley region and speak with a dialect unique to Virginia and North Carolina, called Tuckahoe, a carry-over from 18th century. I make this reference because, during the next few school years, I will find our accent to completely defy the rules of phonetics and spelling.

The Virginia town we live in is small. I enjoy living in a small town because everyone knows everybody else, but it is as much a curse as a blessing, because again, everyone knows everybody else. News and gossip travel fast, although not always accurately, through the community grapevine.

I am round and roly-poly; don't miss many meals, with full cheeks and light skin. My hair color is strawberry blonde, which my grandfather refers to as 'pink' (and is but one of the many injustices

I suffer from the people who love me). My eyes are green and when I smile they deform into two slits, resembling an Asian, but not.

The house we live in is modest, white, with a picket fence around the yard. It was built along with several others for soldiers, like my father, returning home from World War II. It is located right in the center of town, the business district, which consists of a drug store, a soda shop, a barber, cobbler and a Five and Dime. The town actually stretches out for miles and includes a lot of farms. There are a few small local grocery stores where we purchase our staples, like flour, sugar, and tea. The refrigerated section holds the milk, butter, and, of course, the much needed containers of live fishing worms.

Most families in the area raise their own vegetables. Any overstock will be canned or preserved for the approaching winter. Fruit trees are abundant around here, particularly apple trees. Apples are used to make some of the finest apple pies or cobblers, especially when they are topped off with homemade ice cream. Any overstock of fruit, like strawberries and blackberries, are preserved to complement our morning toast or flapjacks. Food, of any kind, is rarely wasted in this town. But a major problem for the population is the lack of refrigeration, so a lot of our meats are cured, smoked or salted. Milk, eggs, and cheese are delivered weekly, by truck, and placed into an insulated box that sits outside on our front porch. On our back porch, we have what is called an ice box, which is exactly what it sounds like, a large metallic box that holds a large block of ice and is used to cool our perishables. During hot weather, we awkwardly, and rather dangerously, use an ice pick to chop off a few pieces from the block to chill our drinks. Hunting is popular among many local men, not only as a sport, but as a means to put food on the table, preferably squirrel or rabbit.

The town, like most in the south, is segregated. There are railroad tracks that run through the middle and serve as a sort of Line of Demarcation, separating the races. The tracks were not placed with the intent to separate. But, because segregation is justified under United States Constitutional law, the tracks, for all intent and purposes, serve as an informal boundary. The separation does provide a certain amount of privacy for both races.

Churches, schools and stores are located on each side of the tracks, further reducing the need for the races to interact, decreasing the likelihood of friction.

Within the community, there are educated blacks: teachers, doctors, and professors. But I am exposed mainly to those who are caretakers, cooks and housekeepers. Their services are essential to an organized white home.

Within the white community there are also varied echelons of white residents: the upper class, which includes the attorneys, doctors and storeowners; the upper-middle class of farmers, ministers and teachers; a large middle class of government workers, discharged servicemen and utility workers; and last, a small conglomeration of uneducated whites, with whom my family does not associate.

We only have a few ways to communicate, via handwritten letters, telegraph wires, for emergencies or instances requiring speedy delivery, and telephone. Our telephone calls are actually answered and connected by a lady who is located in the upper level or our five-and-dime. When calls are to be placed, she answers, and identifies herself as the "Operator." You tell her who you want to speak to and she connects the call, keeping in mind, that not everyone in the community can afford the luxury of a telephone.

The World and Local News is delivered via radio (until 1953 when a neighbor gives us a black and white television set they intended to discard) or through the local community grapevine. But, the preferred source of communication is face-to-face.

Our family operates within a self-described and pre-determined political correctness. Many of its rules and standards were established decades ago by great or great-great ancestors.

The head of our household is my paternal grandfather. He lives nearby and is regarded in the community as a self-made man of wealth and stature. He served on the Town Council for many years and is a member of the Masonic Lodge. His parents were immigrants from Germany and while he can speak the language, he refuses. "I was born an American and so as long as I'm alive, I will only speak English," he proudly states, "and so will you." Grandfather is articulate, handsome and kind, the epitome of a southern gentleman, which requires a polite amount of hypocrisy simply to get along. He is the husband of a one-time local debutante and the father of six successful children. For the most part he is a passive man, most comfortable amidst the tranquility of his apple orchard.

His wife, my grandmother, is largely unpredictable in her mood swings. Born the daughter of an affluent townsman, she revels in her birthright, which she will share with anyone who dares to listen. Her conversations are for the most part irrelevant to current events, but revolve around events or persons long since gone. In her on-going attempt to reclaim her rightful place and popularity amid her ever-changing community, she far-too-often, resorts to sharing petty gossip. She is, though, a devoted mother, aggressive and relentless in her commitment to protect her young.

Father was born into a privileged and loving home. I'm told he was a sensitive child; his true passion was reading. In a small town where most local boys his age did not have the resources to continue their education, he was one of the fortunate ones. Following his college graduation, he immediately enlisted into the Army, proudly serving as part of "The Greatest Generation," those who served in World War II.

Mother is somewhat unique when compared to many of the local women. Born a child of the Great Depression in the dusty Midwest, she apparently had no idea that her childhood was barren when compared to, say, mine. But she says most of her childhood community had suffered the same poverty; therefore, to her, life was normal, she was happy. Never being one to complain, she is proud of her background, the love and commitment of her bare-roots parents who raised her to be strong, curious and independent.

When my entire family, immediate and extended, gathers, there are approximately forty people. Each person fulfills a different, but necessary role in its smooth operation. We get together often, at least once a week, if not more. I have many cousins. Four are girls, two older, one younger than I, but we are near in age, and the babies of the lot. The remaining cousins are older boys, who are expected to counsel us, the girls, by default, based on sex, age and traditional birthright, a carry-over from the nineteen-forties, far as I know. Fortunately for us, they are good guys, thoughtful and generous and just as uncomfortable with the tradition as we.

On Sundays after church, or on holidays, the entire family gathers for lunch at the home of my grandparents. The men always gather in the sitting room, while the ladies always gather in the kitchen, or dining area. The children run outside in delight to play baseball, or perhaps climb the old apple trees behind the house, and playfully harass each other. Harassment is part of our relationship and the preferred way to show our mutual love and affection.

The family is broken down into informal leadership roles. Leadership positions are assigned according to age and supported by the belief that with age, come wisdom and experience. There are three tiers of understood leadership, each designated by age and sex: the senior position is held irrevocably by the elder male until death or dementia, whichever comes first; the second tier is designated to the eldest son, who will someday assume his father's position; the third tier goes to the eldest third generational male, who must

"Yes'm"

also be a direct descendant of the elder, even though that particular person may not want the job. The logic behind these designations is deemed necessary to ensure that within each age group there is one overseer, one voice of reason, a last ditch effort to prevent the family public embarrassment or an individual bodily injury, by all definition, a fall guy. It works quite efficiently as each tier generally moves along in a pack with its leader.

The air of the sitting room is thick with the smoke of cigarettes, cigars and pipes, and a gray cloud looms above. The gentlemen are all leaned back comfortably in their over-sized chairs, one leg crossed over the opposite knee. Upon arrival, the first few minutes are routinely devoted to a polite exchange of greetings and pleasantries. After the ladies depart for the kitchen, the men turn to serious family business. The topics of their discussion may range from which candidate for Town Mayor the family will publically support, to which among them is the best messenger to persuade a certain baseball coach that one of "our" boys should pitch. The conversations are typically agreeable and civilized. But, on the rare occasion they should disagree, the tone is louder and more combative.

The logic behind the need for group agreement is simple: It will send the public message that we, the family, are united in our solidarity. Simply put, the larger the numbers, the more power and influence.

The women are not included in the Sunday decision-making process. The men reason that the handling of business affairs is a difficult and tedious process, simply too heavy a burden for the women to bear. So, in a spirit of generosity, they accept that responsibility as entirely their own. The women do agree to defer involvement in those details, but, most likely, they have no interest, anyway.

In-laws have no influence; their input is politely tolerated but rarely considered.

The field workers and household staff are black employees. Most have had an association with our family for decades. They are well intertwined within the family, providing services, devotion and loyalty, all exhibited in a respectful and subtle manner. A relationship between employer and employee is inconspicuous, but an alliance of sorts is understood. All the workers are paid a daily income and provided with a hearty lunch or dinner, dependent on their work schedule. Some employees, the elderly, the most devoted or the longest serving, might be provided with two meals a day, in addition to their income. On summer days, they all gather to eat at a picnic table placed in the shade of an old tree. When the weather begins to turn cold, they will move to a table that sits outside on a covered porch and tucked away from the elements. Most of the workers are related: mothers, fathers, sisters, cousins. Occasionally, based on the work to be done, they are accompanied by their children.

Fulfilling a vital, though underestimated, role within our self-proclaimed power family is Pearl. Pearl is a God-fearing, uneducated and simple black woman who serves as my caretaker. She makes it her personal mission to deter me from a pre-determined life of self-importance and bigotry. "If you want to change the world, child," she says, "It has to be done one day at a time. Ain't no hurrying about it, takes lots of patience. You listening to what I say?"

1954

Chapter Three

***

- *CBS Morning Show* with Walter Cronkite: Today, May 17, 1954, The U.S. Supreme Court unanimously delivered a ruling in the civil rights case of *Brown v. Board of Education of Topeka, Kansas*. The Court concluded the State-sanctioned segregation of public schools to be unconstitutional. For further details, tune in to our regularly scheduled evening news report at seven. We will now return you to your program.

***

The first few years of my life have been focused almost entirely on illness, tonsillitis. My nights are filled with thermometers, and occasionally, the dreaded enema, an injustice in itself. Because of my fragile state my parents give me a lot of attention and special treatment. I should be attending kindergarten, but because kindergarten is not legally required, and because I have missed more classes than not, my parents plan for me to remain home this school year. The hope is that I will regain my strength in preparation for the first grade. I don't really mind missing school. I'd rather stay home anyway. I don't like waking up early, being rushed to get dressed, only to go out into the weather to a place I don't care about going.

My mother has recently taken a position working for a local utility company, so most days it's just me and Pearl. Mother drives over to Pearl's house each morning before work to pick her up and takes her back home in the evening.

Pearl has been working for our family in varied capacities since she was a youngster. She is now stooped over a bit and shuffles to walk. Her hands shake a little, especially when she reaches out to turn a door knob or pick up a jar. As the days go by it is increasingly difficult for her to get around. She regularly steadies herself on the arm of the couch in her efforts to sit. Her eyes are very watery, bloodshot and almost black, like a deer. Her hair is black, highlighted by threads of gray. She wears it up, braided in the back and wrapped around her head.

Pearl's skin is like black leather, and her fingers are long and thin. Her fingernails are slightly yellowed from the hard work that has taken years from her life. She wears summer dresses year round, all of which rest on the tops of her tied shoes, heavy and black, with thick soles. When the weather is chilly she puts on a sweater, the only one I've seen, light blue, buttoned front, soft. She is slight in stature with a crooked back, hunched forward, which surely makes it difficult to walk and presents itself in a shuffle. Pearl has only two teeth, in the upper front, causing her to constantly suck in her cheeks and release the air, resulting in a *"click."* All dusting, sweeping and folding of laundry, is accompanied by the *clicking*. The sound serves me well. I use it like a radar to home in on her location.

"Pearl," I say as I saunter into the living room, rubbing the sleep from my eyes and in search of that familiar lap where I begin each day. My hair is still ratted and unruly from a long night of sweaty, interrupted sleep. I feel her hands wrap around my waist as she lifts me into my place.

"Yes, child," she says, stroking my hair with one hand.

"I don't feel too good."

"Yes, baby girl, I know. I'm sorry. Your Mama said you had a rough night." She brushes my bangs to the side and rests her hand upon my forehead. "Oh, baby girl, you burning up!" she shrieks. This has become part of our routine. She knows what to do, and has taken care of this many times. She shuffles as quickly as she can into the bathroom, where I hear the slamming of cabinets in her search for a towel. Soon I hear the squeak of the water faucet as she draws water into the tub. I am waiting in the rocking chair, dreading what I know is ahead. The water turns off and I hear her *clicking* headed my way. She hoists me into her arms, and together, we turn toward the bathroom.

We are standing beside the bathtub when she kneels down and gently wraps her hands around both my arms. She looks into my eyes and says, "Child, I know you hate this, and Pearl hates it too, but I have got to do it for your own good. You do know that, don't you?" I nod, yes, I do.

She peels the flannel pajamas from my body, and my skin is overcome with goose-bumps, shocked to the surface by the cold air. Mumbling to herself and shaking her head gently, she lifts me up over the side of the tub and drops my feet into the cold water. "Sit down, Child," she says softly. I edge my way down into the ice cold water, eyes watery, and teeth chattering. Finally, when I'm submerged waist high in the water, Pearl reaches for a washcloth, places it into the cold water, and strategically rubs it head to toe, hair and all. "Lord, forgive me for what I do to this child." Occasionally she stops the soaking and places her hand on my forehead to check for fever. Once satisfied the fever has dropped, she reaches for the towel that she has hung over the radiator and swaddles me in its warmth. She whispers, "Pearl's poor baby girl. Poor, poor baby girl." I just look back into those warm brown eyes.

Trauma over, and emergency avoided for now, we retreat to the rocking chair. I am still wrapped in my towel and her loving arms. We rock, for hours. I snuggle up close to her, trying to rob her of her heat, and listen as she hums "Jesus Loves the Little Children," a song I've learned in church.

I would spend many days right there in the safety of those arms, rocking, and listening to her hum, telling Bible lessons or the occasional life story. Remarkably, all the stories have the same moral: "I hope you will grow up to be a kind person."

"I'm kind, Pearl!" I insist.

"I know you're kind, but I hope you work real hard never to be mean to anyone, just 'cause they a different color or 'cause they don't have much. Everybody has feelings you know, and they get hurt just the same as yours. Your feelings get hurt sometimes, don't they?" she asks, lowering her head nose-to-nose with mine, smiling.

"Yes, Pearl, they do get hurt sometimes."

"How you like it?" she asks.

"Not very much," I answer.

"Well, you do that for Pearl. Try not to be mean, and it will certainly be one of my biggest blessings. I can't ask for no more than that right there." Finished with the lesson for now, we sink into the rhythmical squeak of the rocking chair.

Chapter Four

It is through Pearl's life stories that I learn she and my father have actually known each other since they were children. Her parents, now deceased, worked for my grandparents. Her father helped with the gardening and yard work, while her mother was my father's caretaker, much as she is to me.

"Oh," she said, "Your Daddy a fine man. Those other children, they were nice enough, but your Daddy, he the best. He had that big old smile and his eyes, oh; they glowed like the gateway to heaven. I can see him yet, just lying in that swing on the porch, all propped up on a pillow, just reading and reading. Oh, and he smart, too. And, your Daddy, well, he never 'tell' us what to do, he 'ask' if we mind doing something for him. 'Course, we would have never said no, but nice to be asked just the same. And when he pass by on his way somewhere, he always gave a nod of his head or a 'howdy do' to everybody along the way."

I look up at her, urging her to continue.

"Well, it's a right long story, but I can tell you a little since we just sitting here anyway. See I'm older than your Daddy. I was about fourteen when I got to know him, talk to him and such, I mean. People didn't talk to their help too much back in those days. It was all business, not like you and me, being friends and such. We workers just did what we were told, and when all our work was done we went on home."

She chuckles, "Well, one day it was so hot outside and your Daddy, he still in elementary school, was rocking in that swing on the porch again, reading another book. Lord, he smart. Anyway, pretty soon he reached down and took a long pull from a *Nehi* orange soda. Oh, it look so good, and Pearl was just a sweating. I was hanging them clothes on the line in the yard when I think I see him kind of looking at me, so I kind of smile, you know, not to be rude is all. Out of the corner of my eye I was watching him drink that soda. See, Pearl's family couldn't afford no sodas, and I don't know as I'd ever rightly had one. Anyway, all of a sudden, your Daddy just jumped up off that swing and ran inside the house. All I heard was that old screen door slam shut behind him and I start to worrying. You know, like maybe he was mad or embarrassed that the help had smiled at him, I didn't know. Some people get mad at that. I was sure hoping that his Mama don't come out of there. Lord, don't want to cross that one."

"What's that?" I tip my head.

Realizing she has misspoken, she quickly follows with, "Oh, what did I say? Forget that," and hurriedly moves forward with her story. "Well, Child, you won't believe what your Daddy had gone and done. He come right back out of that house, headed my way, and he was carrying in his hand an orange *Nehi* soda! I thought, Oh, lord what he going to do with that bottle? But he was still coming my way. I was too scared to run. 'Course he'd have caught me anyway, so I just stood there on the other side of that clothesline, sweating and scared to death. Then that man, your Daddy, well, he got right up in front of me and just stood there. He was staring right at me. Lordy, I wasn't 'bout to move, I was shaking. But then, oh!" Her facial features soften, "He held that cold soda right out to me. He didn't say one word. He was just looking at me like I was stupid or something for not taking it. I guess he got frustrated that I was so slow to respond 'cause then he stretched his arm out closer to me. Lord, that soda was right next to my hand so I had no choice, I grabbed it. Lord, Pearl was so hot. Soon as I take it from him he said, 'You enjoy it.' Lord, and he wanted me to enjoy it! Child, that was the best soda Pearl ever had in her life."

"How you like that story? Let's go out on the front porch and get us some sunshine. Fresh air do you good."

Chapter Five

In all ours years together, I will only be angry at Pearl once. It is one of a very few days when she has grown tired of my incessant chatter. Spring is just beginning to break when she suggests I take a bag of *M&M's* outside and plant them under the mimosa tree out back. I assume if I plant them I will get an *M&M* tree. Particularly, I want a red one, so that's what I am planting. Pearl has not actually said a tree will grow, but the idea is implied. Excitedly, I grab a spoon from the kitchen cupboard and head outside, bag in hand.

I am sitting comfortably in the dirt, in my dress and saddle oxfords, digging furiously with my now bent spoon when my brother comes rushing around the side of the house.

"Girl!" He is standing over me in his plaid shirt and blue jeans, hands resting firmly on his hips, "What in the world do you think you're doing?"

"Planting *M&M's*," I answer, looking up into the bright sun and using one hand to shield my eyes. "I'm going to get us an *M&M* tree!" I respond excitedly. I am sure he'll especially love me for this one because he loves chocolate. I wait for his yelp of delight. Nothing.

"Well, if you aren't the stupidest girl! I just don't know. No *M&M* tree is going to come up out of that rock hard old dirt!" He remains standing over me, now rocking back and forth, his hands in his pockets. "Don't waste your time with that, you hear?"

"Well Pearl said . . ." I get up and brush the dirt off the back of my dress.

"I don't care what she said, no *M&M* tree is going to come up! You're just wasting your time!" That said, he takes off running toward the front yard.

I am humiliated. And I have gotten my dress filthy dirty. I have bent one of Mama's good spoons. And my brother thinks I'm an idiot.

"Pearl!" I yell as I fly through the back screen door. She appears from the kitchen. "You lied to me, Pearl!" I scream. "Here, I thought we were friends! Brother said no *M&M* tree is going to grow up out of that dirt. He said that it was too hard and I was just wasting my time!" With that, I storm into my bedroom to plot my revenge.

Getting back at Pearl doesn't take me long. Each afternoon the *Good Humor* truck frequents our neighborhood selling ice cream. My parents always leave a couple of nickels on the table so I can buy one for me and get another one for Pearl. I am waiting to hear the ringing bells of the truck, and right on time I hear its approach. I run to the window to look outside and see that the truck is still a few houses down. Ours will be next. I keep watching as the truck stops in front of our house, and wait until it has moved down two or three houses more. Then I say, "Pearl! I want an ice cream! And I want you to go get it!" Under normal circumstances I am the one who goes to get our ice cream, but not today.

She steps out from the kitchen, wiping her hands on her apron, and holds out her palm for the nickels. I slap them into her hand and say, "And I want a Fudge Rocket!" She doesn't say a word. She shuffles to the door and down the steps. I watch through the window as she walks along the road. I am amused, for a minute or two.

By the time Pearl returns to the house my senses have returned. I feel guilty, the sick to your stomach kind of guilty, but I'm not about to admit it. She steps through the door and hands me my ice cream (I notice she hasn't gotten one), she sets her nickel back on the table and doesn't utter one single word. She doesn't look at me. She goes straight back to the kitchen.

My original feeling of power stems from the fact that Pearl works for my parents. Should I complain, it is likely, that she will be let go. Pearl knows it too, and she needs the money. This is my first form of malicious blackmail.

I try to enjoy my ice cream when I imagine my mother's voice saying, "I hope you don't choke on it," something she says when she is put out with one of us.

Several hours later there is still no word spoken by Pearl. She is sitting on the couch. I walk up close to her, trying to get her attention. I bend down and look up into her face, smiling. Nothing. I sit next to her on the couch, arm to arm, but she acts like she doesn't even know I'm there. "Pearl," I finally relent, "I'm sorry, okay?"

"Well, you don't sound so sorry. I don't hear the smallest ring of sincerity in there anywhere," she says.

"I am!" I search quickly for a tone that will reflect sincerity. I find one, I think, and in barely more than a whisper, I say, "I am real sorry, Pearl." I give her the under my eyelashes look. My lips are puckered out as I try to look most pathetic. "I am real, real sorry, Pearl." I climb up onto my knees; we are now face to face.

"Well, I don't know. I just don't know. I guess I could forgive you this time. Seeing that's how people learn . . . from their mistakes and all. But suppose your just pulling my leg? I just don't know," she stops to consider. "You know what they say, 'Fool me once, shame on you; Fool me twice, shame on me.'"

"Pearl!" I say, "You got to forgive! You always say that yourself!"

"Well, that's true. I do say that, sometimes. I reckon I'll just have to take a chance and forgive you then," she says, smiling.

"Pearl, that isn't funny. You really scared me. It's wasn't funny."

"Child," she responds, "You need a good scare once in a while. It will do you nothing but good. Come here, give me a hug."

1955

Chapter Six

***

- *NBC Camel News Caravan* with John Cameron Swayze: Today, December 1, 1955, a 42 year old African American woman, Rosa Parks, boarded a City bus in Montgomery, where she refused to surrender her seat to a white passenger as required by law. The event has sparked a city-wide bus boycott. We will keep you aware of any further developments in this story.

***

I finish my breakfast and ask Pearl whether I may go outside. Permission granted.

I bound down the steps and drag my tricycle out to the sidewalk. Just as I begin to climb on, I notice a black man walking up the sidewalk in my direction, so I decide, instead, to sit on the front step of our house to watch him and see where he is going. As he walks by, he slightly tips his head and says, "Good morning." There are no black families in our neighborhood, so I surmise that he is probably going to do some work for one of the neighbors.

"Morning," I respond, watching as he moves along.

I spend the day jumping rope and playing in the yard. My trusty beagle and I climb to the top of our dirt mound in the backyard where we set sail to foreign lands.

Later that afternoon, I see the same man working his way back down the sidewalk, so I run to the sidewalk, too. I notice when he sees me that he crosses the street to the opposite side. Must be a game, I think, so I cross the street too. Now we're both standing on the gravel side of the street. He looks up to see me on his side again and just as quickly returns back to the sidewalk. Naturally, I, too, return to the sidewalk. This time though, he smiles a little, and maintains a steady pace in my direction. As he nears me I hear the screen door slam and turn to see Pearl step out onto the front porch. "Child, Lord a mercy, what are you doing?" she yells. "You just get yourself up here, right now!"

"I'm just playing with this man walking down the street," I defend, remaining on the sidewalk.

By this time, the man is standing right beside me. Now we are both facing Pearl.

He smiles and tips his hat, "Well, morning, Miss Pearl."

Pearl brushes down her dress with her hands and says a quiet, "Oh, Hello, Calvin. I'm so sorry if she's bothering you. I never know what this one's going to do, everything a game."

"Pearl," I yell, looking up at Calvin for confirmation, "It was a game!"

"She's fine," he says, coming to my defense, "Ain't no trouble, Miss Pearl. No trouble at all." That said, he straightens up and moves on down the road.

Pearl scolds, "Girl, you best get yourself up here right now!"

"Why are you yelling, Pearl? You don't need to yell at me for crying out loud. You mad? Why you mad?" I ask, "We were just playing a game. Kind of like tag."

"Girl," she says, "That weren't no game of tag! And he weren't playing! You best get up here right now!" she is flailing her arms through the air, encouraging me to come. "One day," she says, "you're going to start a whole lot of trouble 'round here and somebody else is going to get hurt 'cause of it!"

I reluctantly go to the porch where I climb up onto the front porch swing. Pearl sits down next to me and tries her best to explain to me two very foreign concepts: the interaction between the races, and the act of kidnapping. This discussion will leave me with a monumental change in perspective. One I will surely never forget.

"Child, listen to me. Pearl's not mad. She scared. There's a difference. You cannot be going up and talking to people you don't know, number one. Not all people are nice. Most are, but not everyone, so you mind that. You hear me?" I nod. "I don't want to scare you, but seems somebody's got to put some fear in you just to slow you down. Sometimes children get stolen. Why I remember back in 1932 this beautiful little baby boy was taken in New Jersey. And, God bless his heart, he didn't never come home. If someone should take you away from your Mama, Daddy, and me," she says, "Lord, we would all just shrivel up and die." She pulls me close.

"Second," she reaffirms her stern look, me still in her arms, "You listen good. Cause' I don't never want to tell you this again. But it's for your own good, and everyone else's. Some white folk don't like black folk, at all, period, just 'cause they black. That's reason enough." I sit in silence trying to take it in. "And, some white folk don't want their white children even near somebody that's black. They get really mad. And when those kind of white folk get really mad, they can start a whole lot of trouble for a whole lot of people. Somebody could get hurt." She looks down at me. "Now maybe you don't understand, but I'm asking you, don't do that again. Don't you put nobody in that position. You hear me?"

"I won't, Pearl. I didn't mean to," I answer.

"I know you didn't, Child, I know," she says, resting her head against mine.

Chapter Seven

"What's your name?" I ask as I sit on a concrete block, eating *Cheerios* and focusing on the man hired to dig out our basement.

"Raymond," he mumbles, focused on his work at hand. He is so dark I can barely see his eyes, and he's huge, built like a prize fighter. He doesn't talk very much. It's like pulling teeth to try and carry on a conversation with him.

Pearl told me I could sit here and watch him work, but I am not to talk him to death or go into the hole that he's digging.

"How come you're working so early?" I ask.

"Cooler in the morning," he answers.

I watch time and time again as he places the heel of his foot onto the shovel and uses all his muscle to thrust it deep into the ground. Slowly the wheelbarrow fills, and he empties it into a pile behind the shed, my ship.

Religiously, each day at noon he leans his shovel against the house and reaches down for the brown paper sack that holds his lunch. Bag in hand, he walks over to the picnic table under an old maple tree with his plans to eat his sandwich, enjoy the shade, and probably, get some quiet.

"Yes'm"

For weeks he comes to the house. The hole that started beside the house is getting wider and deeper. Making progress, he is eventually under the house, now supported by the placement of sturdy wooden beams, and he is no longer visible from my position on the concrete block. I roll my block to as near my specifically defined boundary as I can. I am almost under the house, but not quite, right on the edge.

"Miss Sammie," he warns, "I think you best move that block further away from the house. These beams just might give out." Stubborn, I don't budge. I scuff my shoes in the dirt, looking away from him.

"Well, I can't talk to you if I'm so far away," I point out.

"Yes'm," he answers, now at the entrance, leaning against the shovel. He's quiet for a moment, searching for a better approach.

"Miss Sammie," he continues, "You ever see that movie, *The Wizard of Oz?*"

I perk right up, "Yes, I did, it is really good." I am absolutely thrilled that he wants to talk to me.

"Well, did you see it when that house fell on the evil witch?"

I run inside.

Chapter Eight

As quickly as I awake, I am in motion. My footie pajamas scuff against the floor as I walk from my bedroom to find Pearl rocking in the chair. She assists as I crawl up into her lap.

"Good morning, child," she greets, "You want some breakfast?" No, I shake my head, not yet. Oh, what we going to talk about this morning? Let's see," she asks, rocking. "Well, um, oh, I know. Let's talk about Raymond since he's here. See, Raymond is my brother. I have two, both younger than me. My other brother is named Edgar. Raymond is close to your Daddy's age and real gentle. But Edgar, he the baby, the older he gets, the meaner he gets. You'll know him when you see him 'cause he has a gold front tooth."

She goes on, "Both my brothers and I used to work off and on at your grandparents' house to earn a little extra money. I remember one day while I was there, up on the porch cleaning windows, I saw your Granddaddy's old plow horse lay right down on the ground and refuse to get up. That horse laid down right under one of those old apple trees. Oh, Child, your Granddaddy was just beside himself. He'd had that horse a long time. I can close my eyes and see it yet. Your Granddaddy out there trying to coax old Barney to stand up, but it weren't to be. Pretty soon your Daddy saw what was going on and he run off down the driveway to the barn. Then he come running back with two big canvas straps. He climbed up high into that tree and hooked those straps around a limb. Then he climb back down and lie on the ground, right next to that horse, trying to wiggle the other end of those straps underneath that horse. Anyway, your Daddy, he was just a working, but the horse was just too heavy. So he looked around for somebody to help him, and he saw Raymond over working in the garden. Your Daddy yelled and Raymond he come a running. Pretty soon Edgar come tearing around the side of the house too. You hungry yet?" she interrupts. No, I shake my head.

"All right," she continues, "Where was I? Oh, Edgar running to help. Just like your Daddy, Raymond and Edgar both dropped to the ground next to that horse and they worked until sure enough that strap came out on the other side. Then your Daddy, he climb back up into that apple tree where he was just a pulling on those straps. They worked near all day and even used a tractor to try to get that horse pulled up onto its feet, but it didn't work. Finally, they just left Old Barney on the ground and sat with him till he gone." She paused to shake her head at the memory. "Ever since then, they've been good friends." She looks down at me and is shocked to see that I'm crying.

"Lord, Child," she wipes away my tears with her hand, "Pearl didn't mean to make you cry. I'm so sorry. I thought you'd like that story."

"I do like it, Pearl. I just don't like the part where the horse died."

"*Ah,*" she consoles me, "Come. Cuddle up. You want Pearl to make you some of her special waffles this morning?" I nod, yes. "Okay, when you quit your crying, I'll make you some." My feet hit the floor.

1956

Chapter Nine

Today it is really snowing outside. Pearl stands by the window looking outside. "Oh, child," she says, "Just look at that snow. It's beautiful, and coming down pretty hard."

"Can I go outside?" I ask.

"Not yet, your Mama said you need to practice writing your letters. She takes me by the hand and together we walk over to the dining room table. While I climb up into a chair, she places a writing tablet in front of me. "Okay," she says, "Now do a big 'A'." I reach over for my newly sharpened No. 2 pencil and begin, resting my elbow on the table. "Capital A," I say, using my tongue to direct my hand; now, "little a," I say, my tongue swirling in motion. Pearl has a copy of the letters that Mother drew for her to use as examples. "That one ain't right," she says. "It don't look like your Mama's." I erase it and start over. "Okay, that's better. Now do the next one," she instructs.

Before beginning the next letter, I tear a page of paper from the notebook and scoot it over to Pearl. "Here, Pearl, you do it with me."

"Child," she says, "Pearl can read and write! What you think?"

"Well, I know, but it won't hurt for you to practice some."

"I will later, child," she says, "I got to get your lunch. I put it in the oven to get warm. Should be done by now." She shuffles off to the kitchen.

In a few minutes she returns with my favorite, fish-sticks. "Yum, Pearl, my favorite! Thanks!"

"Is that your favorite? I didn't know that?" she teases, pushing my notebook off to the side and setting the plate down in front of me. I jockey around her arm for the fork and throw the napkin off to the side.

"Where are your manners? Where does that napkin go?" she asks, sternly. I reach across the table, grab it, and slam it down onto my lap. I can't answer my mouth is full. "That's better," she praises. I nod and chew.

While I enjoy my lunch with Pearl sitting beside me working on her letters, there is a knock at the front door. "I'll go," she says. I watch as she works her chair away from the table and shuffles through the living room toward the front door. She has barely opened it when it is pushed in harshly from the outside. "Lord, Missus," I hear Pearl say, so I climb out of my chair and peek around the corner. I see my Grandmother push her way inside. She is throwing her short arms around in an attempt to remove the snow from her coat and blue hair.

Pearl shoots me a "What is she doing here?" glance, but I don't know, so I shrug my shoulders in response. We wait.

Between the living room curtains I can see that my Grandfather is waiting outside in the car, so I know that whatever this is, it won't take too long. Duly cleared of snow, Grandmother looks up and I am struck to see her sour little turned-down mouth. She moves closer to Pearl.

"What are you doing in the house while my grandchild eats her lunch?" Grandmother challenges Pearl. *What she usually does while I eat my lunch, sit next to me.* But I stand mute. In this rare instance the saying, "Children are to be seen and not heard" works to my benefit.

Grandmother then steps closer to Pearl, who is now hanging her head down, as if inspecting her toes. She makes no eye contact. I have never seen Pearl in a threatened position, but I have had the occasion to know how she feels. I know, from experience too, that these conversations usually get worse before they get better. I edge my way just inside the room. Apprehensive about the way this is going, it occurs to me that I should probably call my mother. But, I fear, the phone is too near the action and I may be grabbed . . . So I don't.

Grandmother is holding a paralyzing glare on Pearl. "You do know when little white children eat their lunch you are supposed to go outside, don't you?" she dares.

"Well, yes'm, I do, but . . ." Pearl tries, unable to finish her explanation.

"Well, you just get yourself outside. And stay there until she's finished eating!"

I am still standing at a distance. I watch as Pearl sits down to put on her heavy black shoes. I watch as she reaches to retrieve her tired little sweater from the arm of the chair. I am dumbfounded.

Just as Pearl takes her first step toward the door I attempt to make a pathetic plea to my grandmother. "Grandma, I am finished eating anyway. It's ok if she stays inside."

That's when the creature turns to face me. I feel a chill run down my spine. "She will do as I say!" she snaps.

Now I have no idea what to do. I'm insulted. I'm terrified, but mostly, I'm . . . I'm . . . angry. It takes me a few minutes to realize exactly what it is I feel. I take a second to weigh my options.

Pearl is taking another step toward the door when I yell, "Pearl! Don't you go anywhere! This isn't her house!" Pearl is stunned by my tone, and stops to look at me. I, too, am stunned by my tone, and feel sick to my stomach.

I try to appear bold, as I cautiously work my way around the room, staying close to the walls. I edge nearer to the door, mindful to leave enough room that I can get away, need be. I slide into a small space behind a chair that separates me from my Grandmother, and stretch my fingertips out to turn the doorknob. With the door open just a crack, I turn, "Grandmother, you best go on home." I hold my arm out toward the door, encouraging her to leave. "Mom and Dad know that Pearl stays in the house while I eat. They don't care. You just go on home." Her expression changes immediately. She looks at me as if I have struck her. In that moment, I feel sorry, and confused, but am relieved when she turns to leave. I am shaking as she passes quietly through the door, slamming it behind her.

The house is eerily quiet when I look over at Pearl. My heart is still pounding in my throat and I feel weak at the knees. Pearl is wiping the sweat from her brow with a red handkerchief and making her way toward the couch. I wait, to give us an opportunity to regain our wits.

"Pearl, are you all right?" I ask from my position near the door, frozen behind the chair.

"Yes, child, I'm all right," she says, working with a pillow behind her.

"Pearl," I say, "I am sorry for what she said to you. She's just a mean old woman who doesn't know any better."

"I don't want to start no trouble between you and your grandmother, Child," she says.

"I know, Pearl. But she doesn't like me anyway. I've never done anything to her, she just doesn't like me. Saying I'm spoiled and such." Pearl smiles and tilts her head, questioningly. "Just saying," I continue, "Just want you to know that it's not your fault."

"Yes'm," she says, "I'm sad for her."

"Why should you be sad for her, Pearl? She's mean. She was mean to you and, she's mean to me. And I'm her blood!" I stop raving a moment to consider my next statement, "Well," I continue, "You can feel bad if you want, but I'm not."

"Ah, now," she scolds, "You're supposed to turn the other cheek when someone does something to hurt you."

"Who on earth says that?" I ask, skeptically.

"Ain't of the earth," she says, "The Bible says that. It says you're supposed to 'turn the other cheek' and forgive someone who hurts you. Says some people are mean 'cause deep inside they're hurting themselves. Says we need to help them, you know. Be kind and understanding," she looks at me, waiting for a response.

I take a moment to find some logic in her statement. Unconvinced, I change the subject.

"Pearl, do you reckon she's coming back?" I ask, moving toward her.

"I doubt it," she answers, "I know I wouldn't come back. Child, you were kind of scary. I'm sure I saw your Daddy in those eyes," she reaches out to poke my cheek.

"Yeah," I slightly tremor, "I was real scared."

"Yeah, me too," she acknowledges.

We remain silent for a few minutes, each replaying the event in our minds like a film. I watch as Pearl occasionally shakes her head, trying to jar the confrontation from her mind.

I, tragedy averted, throw myself down on the couch beside her.

"*Whew*, Pearl," I say, "I think we just cheated fate."

"Lordy," she shrieks, "Girl, we sure did!"

"Uh-oh, the door," I say, now running over to lock it.

Chapter Ten

It's Sunday and we are loading up into the old Plymouth. Mom is wearing a blue feather hat with a veil that dips slightly down over one of her eyes. Dad looks very dapper in his suit and shiny shoes. I am in yet another frilly, itchy dress with the required crinoline, rubbing my skin raw underneath. Pearl is not with us. She typically spends Sundays with her family.

We arrive at church and begin to climb the stairs leading to the sanctuary. My father is following behind my mother, acknowledging friends and shaking hands.

We arrive at our usual pew. It takes two to hold our family. Seated in the back pew are my cousins and brother. The front pew holds the older family members and me. I have to sit next to my parents because they say I squirm around. Sitting to my far left is my grandfather, then my grandmother, my father next to her, my mother and me.

We are just settled in when I hear, "All rise" from the pulpit. The minister, Papa Roles, enters from a side doorway. He is dressed in a shiny robe with a gold scarf draped around his neck. The sun is streaming in through the side stain-glass windows, reds, gold, blue, and a painting of the Lord's Supper is in the background, mystical.

Papa Roles places his hands on both sides of the pulpit, leans forward and bows his head, "Let us pray." The congregation bows their heads in unison. I, however, cannot keep my eyes closed. I have to look around and see who else may be peeking. I wave to my cousin and best friend, Patsy, behind me. She smiles and waves back.

"Amen," he concludes, followed by, "Please be seated." There is the usual rustling of fabric as people move to sit down. His sermon begins with a message of goodness, kindness and mercy and closes with the usual reminder that each of us will undoubtedly face two end-of-life alternatives, Heaven or Hell. He warns that how we choose to live this life will determine the final outcome. He emphasizes that we should not leave outstanding issues unresolved until tomorrow, because a tomorrow is not promised. Suddenly it hits me! I HAVE an unresolved issue! The altercation I had with my Grandmother. Quickly I scoot forward in the pew. My legs squeak as they stick to the years of wax. Arriving at the edge, I lean forward to peer around my parents at my grandmother.

She turns only her eyes in my direction. Her nose is pointed toward the sky and her mouth looks like she just ate a persimmon, sour. We lock in on a sideways glare. Her blue eyes warn me that I had best remain quiet. Mine answer that I am not the one who should be afraid. I hold my position at the pew's edge. We are locked in a visual stand-off when I feel my mother place her hand against my shoulder and nudge me back deep into my seat.

"Sammie, don't. Sit back," Mom whispers.

"But . . . Mom."

"Yes, I know, honey, I know." She pats my leg softly.

"She ought to say sorry," I whisper, mostly to myself, but loud enough that Mom can hear. Mom pats my leg again. She heard me.

After church we drive to my grandparents' house. Patsy and I are playing in the field of apple trees. I love to climb the trees. They are twisted and have perfect branches for sitting or swinging. Patsy is a little overweight, so she cannot pull herself into the trees. We carry on a conversation as she sits in the grass below.

We are just talking about kid stuff when I hear the screen door slam at the house. Shortly, our grandmother appears from around the corner. She is moving quickly considering her short little legs. She has her index finger pointed at me, "You help your cousin get up in one of those apple trees."

I weigh about half of what Patsy does, so I respond, "I can't, she's weighs too much."

"Well, you just best figure out some way," she scowls, and turns stomping back toward the house.

I climb down from the tree and look around for a tree with lower branches. Across the field I see one that may work.

"Come on," I direct. Patsy stands up to follow me.

At the tree, I get down on all fours so she can step up onto my back to reach the first branch.

"Sammie," she says, "You don't have to do this."

"No, you're the favorite. If I don't get you up into that tree I'll never hear the end of it. Let's just do it, get it over with. It's okay."

"Sammie, it's all right, really. I don't care."

"Come on! Get up!" I encourage.

Patsy carefully places her foot on my back, steadying herself against the trunk to offset her weight. I feel my spine bend a little. "Thank goodness," I say to her, as she reaches the lowest hanging limb and pulls herself up. "You weigh a ton!" She responds with her infectious giggle. I watch as she climbs higher and higher, "Okay," I yell, "Now you're just showing off." And turn to leave.

The sun is beginning to sink for the evening when Grandmother steps out onto the porch and calls for all the children, "Time for supper!" We all run from different directions.

Once inside with everyone seated, we note the empty chair that is usually occupied by Patsy. She has not yet arrived.

"Where's Patsy?" Grandmother says to me, her fat hands on her hips. The rest of the family is seated around the dining room table, unaware of our earlier conversation outside.

"I don't know," I say, "probably still in one of the trees you told me to put her into." Now I see my mother smirking from across the table. She lowers her head. She knows where this is going.

"You know she can't get down!" Grandmother spews.

"Well, you just told me to get her up there. You didn't say I had to stay to get her down." Grandmother's face is twisted and beet red. The family members around the table strain to silence their laughter, which only angers her more. She turns and charges through the kitchen and out the screen door. I assume to the apple trees. Now, I think, you have to figure out which one I put her in.

Chapter Eleven

"Here," Pearl says, handing me the Sears Roebuck catalog, "Your Mama wants you to look through here and make a list of what you want for Christmas."

The catalog is thick and heavy, so I lie down on the floor and begin to review the toy section. I begin a list of all the wonderful toys I hope Santa will bring. Finished, I realize it is way too long and reality begins to set in. I know Santa will limit his delivery to one toy, accompanied by what I need, not necessarily what I want. So I shorten the list to include only my favorites.

"Pearl, what do you want for Christmas?" I turn to look at her.

"Oh, just a few kind words," she answers, looking down at a magazine.

"No, really, what do you want?"

"Miss Sammie, although I know you don't realize it, Christmas ain't about what you get. Christmas is about what you give."

"That's what I'm trying to ask you, Pearl, what do you want?"

"Lord, Child, you is thick today. It's not about presents. It's about what you do for others, like the Baby Jesus done for you. It's about helping people who need help or offering a kind word to someone who may just need to hear a kind word 'cause they down and out, that sort of thing."

"So are you saying if I give you a present you aren't going to take it?"

"No, I'll take it 'cause you gave it to me and I love you, but I'd rather have you give me a big old hug than a present. You know, something that only you can give me and nobody else."

"Oh, well, then that's all I want from you too, just a hug, but I hope I get presents from everybody else."

"Yes, I'm sure you do," she laughs.

Each Christmas Eve Dad and his brothers go into the woods to cut Christmas trees, pine and sticky. One of my uncles, the strong-backed member of the lot, then delivers one tree to each family member, my aunt, my uncles and my grandparents.

Our tree has arrived, filling the corner of our living room. "I love the smell of pine," Mom says, every year. She and I are stringing popcorn that we will soon wrap around the tree; Dad stands on a wobbly wooden ladder, adding strands of colored lights; and Brother, gasps for air, as he sprays canned snow foam onto the snowflake shaped window stencils. On the coffee table sits a plate of cookies that Pearl and I made earlier today. The Christmas spirit is in our house.

I am particularly excited about this Christmas because tonight I am to be in the holiday pageant at church. Patsy and I are to be angels. Mom has sewn my costume, as best she can, and Dad made my wings out of a piece of cardboard covered in aluminum foil. My halo is shaped from a coat hanger covered in gold tinsel. Dad stapled two elastic straps to the wings where I will slip in my arms to hold them on. I am ready.

The moment arrives! I am at church and fit nicely into my wings and halo. My aunt, who is at the piano, quietly waves the procession of children onto the stage. I am standing in the very front row, next to Patsy. We have strict instructions not to tease or irritate the other. The music begins and we break into a glorious rendition of "Oh, Christmas Tree." As we finish and prepare for the next song Patsy turns to whisper in my ear, but as she does so, she bumps my wing and breaks a strap. "Great, Patsy," I whisper in a subdued rage, "Now I'm lop-sided."

"Sammie," she says, "I'm sorry. I didn't do that on purpose."

"Yes, you did. Besides that you should have been more careful," I admonish.

My eyes begin to blur from the build-up of tears that slowly make their way down my face. I am fighting to maintain control when I hear a familiar voice, my brother, off in the distance.

"Aunt Tessie," he yells, "Just hold everything for a minute! Just hang on a minute!" I look up to see that he is speeding down the aisle, throwing his hands up into the air.

"Yes, my little darling," she replies in her sing-song voice.

He jumps onto the stage and utters more to himself than anyone else, "Sometimes people just don't think. Something like this can scar a person for life. Guess somebody's got to do something. May as well be me." I watch as he squeezes in between Patsy and I and crouches down. Once stabilized, he reaches up to support my broken wing.

"All right, Aunt Tessie, now!" he yells, "Go!" The music begins once again.

"Yes'm"

I begin to sing, but I am looking down at my hero. "Thank you," I mouth.

Modestly, he rolls his eyes and says, "Ah, Geez, Sammie. Just sing. For God's sake, just sing!"

Chapter Twelve

"I'm going to the five-and-dime for *Vitalis*!" Dad yells through the house. I hear my brother quickly descending the stairs. I just as quickly, hoping for a handful of penny candy, forfeit *The Lone Ranger,* and run toward the door.

"I'm only running in for a minute," Dad says. "You are welcome to go, but you will have to wait outside in the car."

"OK," we reply disappointed, as our vision of the candy jars vanish.

Dad drives through town and in a few minutes he parks the car near the store and gets out.

"OK, I'll be right back," Dad says as he exits the car.

I am sitting in the huge backseat with my feet hanging over the edge. My brother is standing next to me, perched on the hump, so he can see the comings and goings around town.

I notice my shoe lace is hanging so I bend down to retie it, entirely focused on my task.

"Get down!" my brother yells. I feel him place his hand on the back of my neck, and suddenly I am thrust to the floorboard of the car amid the popcorn, graham cracker pieces and a few pennies. I am fighting to get up, like a wet cat, scratching and clawing. So he stands on me, as he stretches out hurriedly over the front seat to push down the locks to the car doors. I note that his feet are barely on me as he struggles to reach the final lock. That is when I make my move. I am about halfway up before he throws me back down and lies on top of me. Now I'm hissing mad.

"Have you lost your mind?" I demand, "Get off me! Let me up!" I growl, still fighting.

"No," he says, "I can't. You have got to stay down, Sammie! I am serious, you just stay down girl!" I note the quiver in his voice and reluctantly relent. We are lying quietly on the floor. He whispers, "Be real quiet. Don't you move one little inch. Something really bad could happen to both of us if you do." We are silent. I am waiting for, well, I don't know.

A few minutes later he slithers up the back of one of the seats to peek over top. "Okay," he says, "it's clear. He's gone. You can get up now."

"What the heck is the matter with you?" I say, "Throwing me to the floor and all! Who do you think you are, anyway?" I thrust myself on to him, just trying to get a little piece of him. I know I'll lose, but I can dream.

"Well, if you'd calm down for a minute I might tell you," he leans in close to my face.

"OK, tell me then." I cross my arms over my chest.

"It was Edgar," he says. I freeze.

"You ever heard about old Edgar?" he asks. "He is real black and got a gold tooth. Oh, people say he's mean, Sammie, real, real mean." I, in the meantime, recall what Pearl had said about Edgar being so mean.

"Sure enough, Sam. He was coming down the street. Headed right toward our car! One of the kids at school told me that HE EATS little white children for lunch! And I'm not joking! That's exactly what they said, and just like that, 'HE EATS little children'!" He holds his hands in front of my face, palms up, "Honest, Sam, that's the truth. I figured I'd best lock the doors unless, of course, you like the idea of being his lunch?" he teases.

"No. Next time, just tell me," I say. What's taking Daddy so long?"

—∞—

"Pearl!" I yell out as I enter the house.

"What is it?" she asks, as I run into the kitchen.

"Edgar! Pearl! I mean Pearl, we saw Edgar at the store!"

"Goodness, slow down a minute!" she says as she continues to steadily peel carrots over the garbage can.

"Well, he was going to eat us for lunch! He was headed right to our car!"

"Oh," she scoffs, "He wouldn't eat you two. You're both way too skinny and tough. I suspect he'd spit you out, both being so spoiled rotten and all. You'd probably make him sick." I am shocked by her apparent lack of concern, so I step around where I can better make my point. Perhaps, I think, she doesn't understand the severity of the situation. "Pearl." She turns away.

"Pearl," I say again. "Look here. Look here, please. I'm trying to tell you something."

"Can't, child," she says, "I'm busy," she is still looking away from me and still peeling.

"Pearl, turn around so I can talk to your face. That's rude you know? I'm trying to tell you something." She reluctantly places the knife and carrot on the counter and slowly turns in my direction. Now fully visible, I see that her hand is over her mouth and tears are streaming down her face.

"Pearl? You crying?" I ask.

"No, child," she says, "I'm not crying. Well, yes, I am, but not cause I'm sad." She bends forward at the waist and places her free hand on her knee.

"Pearl, you sick?" I ask, "I'm going to get Mama."

"No, Miss Sammie. Just give me a minute," her hand still clasped against her mouth. I stand nearby and wait as she struggles for control. "Child, wait just one minute," she says, and draws in a deep breath. "Child," she begins once more before giving up the effort. Now I am afraid, I wrap my arms around her legs. "Pearl," I wail, just moments before she bursts out in hysterical laughter.

"You should have seen your face!" she gasps. I step back. "When you come running around that corner your eyes were big as saucers!" She is completely overcome. "Edgar is mean, but far as I know he hasn't eaten anybody, yet!" She squats down near to the floor, weak with laughter.

"I guess it don't matter to you that I was scared, Pearl," I say sarcastically, stepping back, hands on my hips.

"Sorry," she says, straining to compose herself. "Now tell me. What I want to know is what, just 'xactly, did that big brave brother of yours do when he saw Edgar coming?" She is composed for the most part.

"Well," I begin, "He knocked me down on the floor and . . ." again, she interrupts me, overcome with laughter and crashes the few remaining inches to the floor. "Oh, child," she laughs. "Thank you so much."

"For what? For almost getting eaten? 'Cause you find it so funny that I was scared to death?"

"No, child, for the best laugh Pearl has had in a very long time. Now come over here and help me get up off this floor. If your Daddy sees me he'll think I've lost my mind."

1957

Chapter Thirteen

The first grade! This morning my mother is going into work a little late to make sure I am properly dressed and ready to go. I will attend class for the first half of the day.

Pearl finishes ironing my dress and holds it up for review. It looks stiff as a poker. While Pearl looks on, Mom begins to pull the dress down over my head and finishes by finessing the perfect bow in the back. The only saving grace is that at least I don't have to wear a crinoline. I slip my lace-socked feet into my new patent leather shoes and Mom spins me around so she can brush and comb my hair. Next, she pulls it back into a pony tail and, as a finishing touch, adds a matching bow. At last, I am ready so I stand back for further inspection and do a slight curtsey for good measure.

"Sammie, you look so cute!" Mom announces.

She grabs my hand and pulls me into the living room toward the front door. "Sammie, you only go to school for half the day, so Pearl will make your lunch when you get home. Okay?"

"Yes, ma'am," I reply.

"And," Mom continues, "Pearl is going to be walking with you half way to the school. When you reach a certain point, where you can see the school from the road, she is going to let you go and you will finish the walk by yourself. Okay?"

"Yes, ma'am."

"Sammie, look at me and please pay attention." Her bony fingers pinch my cheeks as she swivels my head in her direction. "When you leave school for the day don't you dilly-dally around because Pearl will be waiting for you right where she leaves you this morning, understand?"

"Yes, Mama, I understand." Convinced I have all the necessary instructions, Mom stands and moves away from the door. At that point Pearl walks over and takes my hand, and we head outside.

We don't talk very much as we walk toward school. I am trying to focus on where, exactly, I am. Just in case I have to come home by myself. When we reach the top of one hill I can see the school off in the distance. The elementary school is located on the other side of the railroad tracks.

Pearl stops walking and releases my hand. Slowly she bends down so we are eye to eye. "OK, Miss Sammie, here we are. This is where I let you go, and that right there," she points to it, "is the school. You see it, don't you?"

"Pearl, yes, I see it! It's right there." Now I point, and check to make sure she's looking.

"OK, now you walk on. You have to cross one street, so be sure to look both ways before you cross. Then . . . look at me. You got to cross those railroad tracks. Be sure to look real good because that signal don't always work right. Child, I said look at me!" She places her hands on the sides of my face to force my focus. "Now make sure a train ain't coming. Please . . . listen to me. If there's a train, I don't care if it's just sitting there, you don't cross. You may think it's stopped, but it ain't. After school Pearl will be waiting right here in front of Mrs. Culver's house. See that flag in her yard? I'll meet you right here after school, right in front of that flag. You got it?"

"Yes, Pearl, I've got it!"

"Now, you be a good girl and show them how smart you are. Don't you get yourself into no mischief 'cause you'll upset your Mama."

"Okay." I turn to begin my solo. Every few feet I turn back to see if Pearl's still there. Yes, she is, she waves me on. "Go on, Child. Get to getting."

As I enter the classroom, I see that there are about fifteen children already in place behind desks. I recognize a few from the neighborhood or church, but not many. I pick a desk near the middle of the room and reach down to straighten the back of my dress to avoid wrinkles, just like Mama told me.

Soon the teacher enters the room. She welcomes us to her classroom and begins roll call: "Tommy, Alice, Bo, Samanthalee?"

"Yes, ma'am, I'm here, but, no, ma'am, it's not Samanthalee. They call me Sammie." I smile my sweetest smile and wait for acknowledgment.

The teacher reaches up and slides her glasses down from the bridge of her nose and peers over them at me, "Well, I beg your pardon, but the roll specifically says your name is Samanthalee."

"Yes, ma'am, it is, but people call me Sammie."

"That's fine, outside of school, but this is a formal setting and here you will be called Samanthalee."

"Well, yes ma'am, that's ok, but if you must say Samanthalee, can you take a breath between the Samantha and Lee, because Lee is actually my middle name."

"Well, the roll shows no hyphenation between Samantha and Lee, so if said correctly it should be Samanthalee."

She continues, "Well, I suppose it wouldn't hurt for me to say Samantha"—she draws in an exaggerated breath—"Lee," and dramatically exhales. With that the classroom breaks out in laughter. I am humiliated and yearn for the security of home.

After school I high-tail it across the railroad tracks to meet Pearl. She is waiting right in front of the flag. Right where she said she'd be.

I throw my arms around her legs, hugging her dress, and say, "I hate school! And . . . . I ain't going back."

"What? Don't you want to learn to read?"

"No. Maybe. Well, I might go until I can read, but then I'm quitting!"

"What on earth happened? You didn't start no trouble did you?"

"I don't know. It wasn't my fault. Honest. That teacher called me Samanthalee, real fast like that, so I told her that my name is Sammie. Anyway, she said she is going to call me Samanthalee anyway, so I said, well can you say, you know, Samantha (breath) Lee, and so then she said, all dramatic and such, Samantha (I drew in a big breath to emphasize the scenario) Lee (slumping over to exhale) and then everyone laughed at me. And that's why I am not going back. It was SO embarrassing." I hear her snicker a little before she reaches out to take my hand.

"And Pearl, it isn't funny! Don't you be laughing." With that, I bend forward to check her expression.

We walk home in silence with me stomping every step of the way.

Later that day, Pearl asks me to repeat my school story for my parents. "Pearl," I say, "you tell them. I told you already. I'm sick of talking about it." I throw myself back into the cushions of the couch to pout.

"No, Miss Sammie," she corrects, "you just sit up straight and tell them yourself. You are going to show your parents some respect and answer yourself, right now. You just sit yourself up and tell them what happened." In a bored monotone I repeat the story, start to finish. At the end, my parents make it clear that I will be returning to school tomorrow, in my clothes or my pajamas, it doesn't matter to them, but, by God, I am going.

Pearl has a difficult time getting me to school today. Unfortunately for me, Mom has instructed her to walk with me right up to the school doors, where she kneels down and takes my hands in hers. "Miss Sammie?" she says, "I want to make sure you know that Pearl is real sorry about how things went for you at school yesterday. If I could change it you know I would, but fact is, I can't, and fact is, you have to go to school, so here we are. Now I just might be wrong, but Pearl would bet good money that you plan to make a break for it once you think I am out of sight? Am I right?" I look up into her eyes, unresponsive. "Yep, that's exactly what I thought," she smiles knowingly. "Anyway, see that house over there?" she points across the street to a two-story white house on the corner.

"Yes," I respond.

"Well, that house, right there, is where Pearl will be spending her day. Right there, swinging on my friend, Nedra's, front porch. I should be able to see these doors pretty good. What you got to say about that?"

"Oh, Pearl," I sigh.

"Yes'm, that's exactly what I'm going to do today, just sit right there on that porch just a rocking and a rocking. So you just go on inside now. Something tells me that today will be a whole lot better." With that she pulls me in for a hug. "You're going to have a real good day."

—⚏—

Again the teacher enters the room and begins roll call again. A few names into the role there is a knock at the classroom door. Mrs. Kyles says, "Enter," and I am pleasantly surprised to see my grandfather enter the room, although I have no idea why he is here. He steps in, removes his hat, placing it against his chest, and leans forward into the face of the teacher. She leans forward to meet him where they trade a soft and short conversation. My eyes are upon them. I see the teacher nod. He bows to her slightly, and leaves. He never once looks my way.

Mrs. Kyles picks up with the roll call right where she left off. "Rebecca, Johnny, Jeremiah, Sammie . . ." I note the room is amazingly quiet so I look up. I see that the teacher is looking straight at me.

"Yes, ma'am?" I inquire.

"You are Sammie, aren't you?" Mrs. Kyles asks.

"Yes, ma'am, I am. I'm Sammie," I answer. That's odd, I think, first my grandfather visits and now the teacher is suddenly calling me Sammie. *Hmmmm.* I wonder if there's a connection. "Present, Ma'am. Yes, I'm here."

Delighted at having survived another school day, I eagerly head for the exit. Pearl is waiting right outside the doors. I grab her hand and start telling her about my day.

"Child, now," she interrupts, "Didn't I tell you today would be better? Someone sure is looking out for you."

"Yes. Pearl, how did you know that today would be better?"

"Simple. 'Cause just when you think you're at the bottom of the pile and it can't get any better, it usually does. Things always look up, child. Sometimes you just have to wait." I nod, amazed by her wealth of knowledge. "Bad thing is," she continues, "You ain't too good at waiting. Maybe you can work on that?"

"Maybe," I say.

"Good. Do I have to walk you all the way again tomorrow?"

"No, I can do it."

"*Whew*," she says. "That is really good news, 'cause that's a mighty long walk for old Pearl." She squeezes my hand.

As I lie on the living room floor, propped up on a pillow, watching *Mighty Mouse*, my personal favorite, I hear, "*Pssst*, Sammie." I turn to glance around the room, but don't see anyone so I return my focus to the cartoon.

"*Pssst*, Sam, over here." Again, I sit up and peer around the room. I see the eyes of my brother peeking around the edge of the hallway entrance.

"What?" I ask, "I'm watching cartoons."

"Just come here," he whispers.

"No, I told you I'm watching cartoons!" I answer, settling back down on my pillow.

"Come on, Sam. Just for one minute. And be quiet."

I begrudgingly rise up off the floor and drag my feet, as if each weighs a ton, over to the hallway. "What you want?" I ask, but see that my brother is now standing at the top of the stairs, in his room. "Why you whispering?" I ask. "You in some kind of trouble?"

"Nah," he answers. "Come on," he signals for me to come upstairs.

"First, tell me what you want. I don't go in your room," I say, suspiciously.

He rests his hands on his hips and says, "Yes, I know. And it was my room last night when you crawled underneath my bed and growled like a catamount. Just come here. I swear, I'm not up to anything." Hesitantly, and against my better judgment, I make the steep climb to his room. As I arrive at the top he scurries over to his 45 rpm record player. "Come on," he says, extending his right hand in my direction.

"What's wrong with you? I am not going to hold your hand!" I declare.

"Sammie, there's a contest at school tomorrow. It's Rock and Roll Day. I want to dance with Candy tomorrow, but I don't know how."

"*Ooooh,* Candy," I mimic.

"Yes, Candy," he answers, shyly looking at the floor. "And I need you to help me practice. I need a partner."

I turn back toward the stairs. "Sammie, come on!" he pleads.

"I don't know how you expect me to help," I respond. "I can't dance either. Wait until Mom gets home. She can dance." In the background blares Elvis Presley and I think I like it.

"Well, I know a little," he says. "Come on, Sam, let's just try," again with the hand. I take it.

"OK, just do what I do," he instructs. He rocks left to right, he steps in and out, he stops a moment to swivel his hips.

"I am not doing that!" I refuse.

"You don't have to. I will," he yells, as he returns to restart the record.

"If Daddy catches you doing that he's going to give you what for," I warn.

He smiles, he knows it's true. He returns to my side, giving further instruction, "It's kind of like a prize fighter. Like, you know, Floyd Patterson. You know who that is, don't you?"

"Of course."

"Well, act like you're Floyd Patterson, just hold my hand while you do it."

Again, we begin, bob and weave, duck and cover. Elvis blares.

"What's going on up there?" Pearl yells from the bottom of the stairs. Brother immediately releases my hand and runs over to the top of the stairs. "Nothing," he yells down the stairs, "We are fine. Go away."

"Oh, no," she yells, "When you tell me to go away that's not what I'm going to do." She starts climbing the stairs.

"Pearl, no, go back down," he yells over the music.

"Why? What are you two up to? I heard some heavy feet stomping going on up here. At first I thought y'all were fighting again, but then I heard the music and decided instead that you might be dancing," she is amused.

"Don't laugh!" he scowls.

"Oh, Lord," Pearl says, as her heavy shoes hit each step. Brother throws himself down on his twin bed, his legs are hanging over onto the floor and his flannel shirt up is high around his chest. I stand still, pending the outcome.

"Look, little Mister, maybe I can help some," Pearls says.

"You can't," he says, placing a pillow over his face. Pearl shuffles over and gently lifts the pillow. "Get up," she says. He reluctantly sits up on the edge of his bed. "I said, get up!" Pearl corrects. Brother rises to stand, swaying in place.

"Now," Pearls informs us, "Believe it or not. I can dance. If there's one thing in the world I can do, it is dance. Now come here. Hold your sister's hand and get ready."

We watch as Pearl makes her way to the record player. "One of you come over here. How's this thing work?"

"Pearl," brother *snorts,* "just forget about it."

"Start the music," Pearl challenges, "And pretend I ain't even here."

"Ain't Nothing But A Hound dog" blares once again through the room.

"Yes'm"

"Now," she says, "I'm going to snap my fingers to the beat. Each time I snap you move your feet, hands, head, or something. We're going to start real slow." She begins snapping and we begin moving our feet, hands, heads and somethings. A few minutes later, Pearl says, "I declare. I think you children got some rhythm!" We laugh, although I'm not sure why.

We wait, watching as Pearl struggles to free herself from a nearby hemp chair with no hemp. Her bottom has sunk through, she's stuck. Finally free and approaching, she says, "Now each of you take a hand. We are going to dance!" She extends her skinny arms.

We laugh as Pearl sings, "Just crying all the time," she bobs and weaves, "You ain't never caught a rabbit," her hips swaying left and right, "And you ain't no friend of mine!" she pulls us in and out. Her long hand is now wrapped around my wrist, forcing my movement.

"Okay," she yells, mid-song, "We are going to all do a little spin on three!" she smiles. Brother and I share a concerned glance. We hope she will complete her little spin on her feet. "Okay, one, two, three," she says, freeing her hands and turning like a ballerina, unhindered by age or the weight of her heavy shoes. Her tired little dress flows around her like a ball gown. She is beautiful.

"Pearl!" I yell, "You CAN dance!"

"Oh, there are a lot of things Pearl can do that you two smarty britches don't know anything about!" she replies, still spinning.

1958

Chapter Fourteen

A middle-of-the-night phone call brings some worrisome news, particularly for Mom. Her father has been transported to Omaha Hospital with pneumonia. A few minutes after receiving the call, my father is on the phone making flight arrangements. The plans are for my brother and me to stay with our paternal grandparents, here in town, for at least a week. We cannot accompany our parents on the trip because we are in the middle of a school year and flights are very expensive.

I am in the bedroom hurriedly packing my Shirley Temple suitcase, "Mom," I yell across the hallway, "I'd rather stay home with Pearl."

"I'm sure you would, but I just spoke with Pearl. We've agreed she should take this opportunity for a vacation. Your father and I thought it would be good for her to rest. She's been looking pretty worn out."

I throw a few more articles in my suitcase, and yell across the hallway, "Mom, who's going to watch the dog while we're away?"

"Oh," she answers, from the distance, "Samson is going with you, but he'll have to stay outside in the barn."

"The barn?" I snarl. "He's used to sleeping with me. He's never slept in a barn before. He'll be scared in there. What if it's cold or rainy?"

"Oh, Sammie, he's a dog. He'll be fine. Besides, that's the least of our problems right now." I agree and return my focus to the job at hand.

A half-hour later, we climb into the car and within minutes arrive at our grandparents' home. The entire yard, twenty acres, is surrounded by a wrought iron fence. The fence serves a dual purpose: it keeps the grandchildren in close proximity and under strict surveillance; and the introduction of any outside interference to a minimum. The house is stately, two tall white columns on the front porch, a long circular gravel driveway. As we approach and the sun is beginning to rise, I see my grandparents descending their front steps.

Mom opens the car door and they speak briefly, wishing her and her father the best of luck. Brother and I exit the car and scurry around to the trunk for our suitcases. Dad meets us there to open it. Time, it seems, is of the essence. I hear a squeal behind me and look to see that Samson is excitedly greeting my grandmother, who has extended her arms high above her head in an attempt to avoid canine contact.

Dad stretches high to close the heavy trunk and sternly reminds us of our behavioral requirements: mind, listen, please and thank you. Mom keeps it short and simple. She kisses us good-bye and says, "We'll be home in a few days. I will call to check on you. Don't aggravate each other."

"Okay, Mama," brother smirks, "We won't."

The four of us stand outside waving good-bye until the car leaves the driveway. "Come on inside," Grandfather says, placing his hand gently between my shoulder blades, nudging me toward the door.

The inside of the house feels empty, lacking the usual bustle of family. The most predominant sound is the ticking of a wall clock. I stop to survey the room, filled with old frames and pictures of people I don't know, a worn oriental rug, two now faded couches with a couple of matching chairs. It feels vacant in comparison to our home, which is small and cozy. I feel out of place. No Pearl. No parents. Cast to the side like an unwanted orphan.

Once inside, my grandmother turns to me with a sweet smile. "Sammie, I'm going to make some flapjacks. Would you like some?"

"No, thank you. It's too early for me, maybe later. You all go ahead though."

I have been here every week of my life but have never slept here before.

"Granddad, where's Samson?" I ask.

"Oh, Gal, I carried him down to the barn."

"Granddad, just so you know, Samson always sleeps with me. Can he please come inside tonight?"

"Nah, Gal, he'll be just fine right where he is. I put down an old blanket for him."

"May I go to the barn?" I ask.

"Yes, that's fine," he replies. "You two kids are real lucky," he continues, "Your Grandma made some of her famous cabbage soup for supper tonight." My brother and I turn to look at each other. We don't like cabbage soup, but we don't say.

Always quick on the draw, my brother says, "If it's all right I think I'll spend the night at Aunt Tessie's down the street." I cut him a death stare. It does sound like a good alternative, but I cannot muster the courage to say, "Me too." I don't want to hurt my grandparent's feelings.

"Okay, whatever. I'm going down to the barn. I won't be gone too long." I head to the door and enjoy leaving the awkwardness behind.

At the barn I struggle to open the heavy doors where I find Samson, tail wagging, glad to see me. I search for a bucket and fill it with water from the outside faucet and pour some food into another. I reach down to give him a few pats on the head. "Yes, you're a good boy."

Never one to look forward to bedtime, tonight I am. I'm already counting down the days. The minutes seem to pass like hours as I sit on the couch in the living room. Grandmother places a wool blanket over me. I can't help but wonder if she put that itchy old thing on me because she loves me or because she wants to torment me.

Finally, darkness falls. One down, six nights left.

"Granddad, where am I sleeping?"

"Upstairs, Gal, in your Daddy's old bedroom."

"Do you think I could sleep downstairs on the couch? I mean Old Man Trouble is up there and I'm scared of him. I don't want him watching me and stuff when I can't see him back." Old Man Trouble is the name of the ghost that lives upstairs. He is actually a deterrent invented by Grandfather to keep the youngsters from sneaking upstairs and getting into mischief. Now he is a problem.

"Oh, Gal," he snorts, "Old Man Trouble ain't interested in you."

"Well, maybe not, but he isn't going to get the chance 'cause I'm not going up there."

"Gal, now you know, if I say you're going up there, you're going up there. You got two choices, hard or easy."

"Easy." I yield. I am so desperate that for a brief second I appeal to my Grandmother for support. Nothing.

Grandfather holds my hand and leads me upstairs into the "Land of the Living Dead." Even the steps creak as we move upward.

I change into my pajamas and crawl into the bed, comforted only by the fact that this was my father's room and he survived. The house is eerie and within the walls are banging noises which Granddad says is the heat. I'm not so sure. The door is closed and I have no night light.

Off in the distance I can hear the howling of . . . Samson. I feel panic build in my throat and bury deep into the blankets.

As if on cue my Grandfather pokes his head through the door. "Did I hear you whimpering, Gal?"

"Maybe a little, but I'm not crying," I answer bravely. "It is kind of scary in here though, and I miss my dog. See, he usually sleeps with me."

"Yea, well you said that, and your Grandma doesn't like any animals in the house, ever."

"Well, he doesn't have fleas or anything. *Pleeeez* . . . let me have my dog?" I flutter my eyelashes.

"No, sorry, rules are rules." He pats me so hard on the head that my neck bends. Then he turns to leave the room. Frustrated, I throw myself back down into the pillows.

"Yes'm"

Sleep comes on and off. At some point in the darkness I wake up and realize I no longer hear my dog barking. *Oh, my God, something has gotten my dog! I should go outside, but its way more scary out there.* I lie back and wait for sunrise.

As I am just about to doze off again, there's another noise from downstairs. *What's that? Sounds like it's coming from the kitchen.* I pull the covers up over my head and stay very still. *Hope whoever it is doesn't know I'm here since I don't live here. They'll get Grandma and Granddad first. Maybe that will give me time to run.* Then the worst thing happens. The door to my room cracks open.

"Gal, *pssst*. Looky here," says a whisper.

I dig my way out from under the covers and see my grandfather. He is holding Samson. I reach out for him. "I'm going to put Samson in here with you, Gal," Granddad says quietly. "But you better make sure he stays quiet 'cause if your Grandma finds out I let him in the house, he and I both will be looking for a place to stay. You able to manage that?"

"Yes, sir," I grin. Samson is turning circles on the bed trying to find a comfortable spot to lie down.

Granddad continues, "At sunrise I'll come back in here to get him and put him back out in the barn. That way nobody except you and me will know he was here. Don't you let on, you hear? Cause if you leak our little secret I'm going to deny it," he says, and he reaches out to pat my head again.

"Yes, thank you. Good night. I love you."

"Me too," he answers, "Night, Gal." The door closes behind him.

One day on the school bus as I return to my grandparents, a boy, Timmy, asks if I can come over to his house and play later. He is a quiet and shy boy. I like him.

"Sure," I answer without giving it a thought.

As soon as I reach the house I run upstairs to change into one of my play dresses and ask my Grandmother if it is okay to go.

"Yes," she says, "but you better be really careful crossing that road. Be back by six o'clock for supper."

I run down the long driveway, come to a quick halt to check for oncoming traffic, and dash across. Timmy has a swing set in his backyard, so that's where we begin. I am delighted that his swing set includes a trapeze. I love to climb. I reach up for the bar, lift my legs, and hang upside down.

Moments later, as Timmy and I are laughing and playing, I believe I hear a faint voice calling from off in the distance, so I drop to the ground to listen. "Gal!" I hear, so I shield my eyes with my hand to look around. "Gal!" I look across the street and can see my grandfather standing in his front yard with what appears to be a pair of binoculars to his face. "Get over here!" he yells.

I immediately run in his direction. Once again I jump the ditch, stop abruptly at the street to look both ways, and bound full speed to his side. "Yes?" I ask, out of breath.

"Gal, you ought not hang upside down in your dress," he scolds.

"Well, what am I supposed to do if I want to hang upside down?"

"Well, just don't hang upside down," he clarifies.

"But . . . . ," that's all that gets across my lips before he grabs me by the hand and drags me toward the old pick-up truck. "Get in," he commands. I reach for the armrest and pull myself up and inside the old truck. We are on the road, but to where I have no idea.

As we arrive in town, Granddad pulls the truck off to the curb and throws the gear into park. I see we are inside the business district. "Get out," he says. I jump out of the truck. Moments later, he is dragging me down the sidewalk by the hand. After a short distance, we enter a men and boys clothing store where a gentleman meets us at the door. "What can I help you with?" he asks. His hands are behind his back.

"You got any coveralls that will fit my granddaughter here?" Granddad asks. "She insists on hanging upside down."

The salesman scoffs and says, "Well, we have some for boys. I suspect I can find a pair that will fit her, but she'll need a shirt or something," the salesman says.

"Okay," Granddad replies, "Give us one of those flannel shirts over there," pointing to a stack across the room.

I am delighted! I sing, "I have pants! I have pants!"

As soon as we return home, I run upstairs to change into my new clothes. Dressed, I run back down the stairs. I plan to return to Timmy's, but as I descend the stairs I see that my Grandmother is sitting nearby on one of the couches. I hesitate when she turns in my direction. "What on earth do you have on?" she gasps. I stand frozen on the bottom step.

"Pants," I hear Granddad reply from his chair where he is reading the newspaper. I can see a slight smirk behind the paper.

"Now, you know young ladies do not wear pants!" she exclaims.

"Well, they do if they keep hanging upside down and showing the world their underwear," he snaps, lowering the paper so he can send her a look. I am still standing in place.

They stare each other down for a few seconds, before Granddad says, "Go on, Gal. Go play with Timmy. You look good." I hit the steps running.

After supper, I head outside. The boys, Brother and our cousins, are building a tree house in one of the old pine trees out front. I, in my new pants, hands in my pockets, saunter up to check out their progress. They have nailed pieces of wood to the tree to serve as steps, so I begin my ascent.

"Get back down," they holler in unison.

"How come?" I say, looking up.

"Because we took a vote! No girls are allowed in this tree house!"

I am immediately insulted. I look down to my side and see that lying next to my foot is a hammer. I take a few moments to contemplate the various services it may provide.

I pick up the hammer and glance up at the tree house. They are preoccupied, laughing and reading comic books, so I prepare to even this field of male domination. I hang the hammer over the front of my coveralls and climb quietly to the top step, where I hook the hammer underneath and pry it loose. It falls to the ground. I look up. There is still no acknowledgment from above. I drop down to the next step and pry it loose. Undetected, I continue with the third and fourth. I work my way all the way down to the ground. They are still clueless.

Done, I stand at the bottom, satisfied, hammer in hand, admiring my handiwork. The wooden steps lie in a heap all around me. Briefly, I remind myself that it will not be pleasant when they get out of that tree.

I continue to stand at the bottom of the tree, quietly considering the consequences of my action, when I hear a squeal from above. I look up to see one of the boy's feet is swinging in the air. He is searching for a step, but there is none. I watch as the others reach down to grab his belt and pull him back into the structure.

"Sammie, what have you done?" Brother says, looking down.

"Can't you see what for yourself?" I look down to the ground, torn, both amused and remorseful.

"Oh, when we get out of this tree . . ." he yells.

"Don't look too good for you all right now." They stare at me from above, stuck.

Feeling pretty good, I turn to go back to the house, and they start to plead.

"Sammie! You can't just leave us up here!" I stop a moment to consider the statement, before I continue to walk away.

The commotion has brought Granddad outside. "Gal!" he yells. "What is going on out there?"

"I don't know," I say, shrugging my shoulders. He walks toward our location and, once he's close to the tree, the boys start to tattle that I have taken their steps down and now they are stuck.

He turns to look at me, "Gal, did you take the boys' steps down?"

No answer.

"Gal, once more. I'm asking did you take these steps down, yes or no."

"Yes sir. I did. But only 'cause they said I couldn't come up in the tree! 'Cause I'm a girl!" I yell upward. "They're stupid anyway. Who cares! Dumb boys! You stupid boys!"

"Yes, looks to me like maybe they are. Stupid, that is." He laughs and looks up at the boys. "Well, I guess," he says, "the next time you boys decide you're smarter than a girl, you better take the hammer with you." I watch, from a safe distance, as Granddad kneels down to inspect the fallen stairs, turning the pointed nails downward. Finally finished, he rises, and motions for me to follow him. As we walk back toward the house, he says, "They'll figure something out." I look up smiling. "They are going to make you pay for this, Gal. You know that?"

"Yes, sir." He reaches out to give me a firm pat on the back.

Indeed, my "sleight of hand" did not go without retribution. I have for nearly two hours been dropped into the bottom of a six foot deep window well along with the remains of dead baby birds and wet smelly leaves. I know that my presence will not be missed until dinner time when my chair is empty. I make myself comfortable and settle down into the leaves. Yes, I think, I am alone in a dark window well for who knows how long. I wonder if I made a wise choice when I confronted the boys. If I had it to do over, would I do it again? Knowing the outcome? Yes, I would, hands down. It was so worth it! I recline against the moist brick to serve my time.

"*Pssst*, Sammie," an echo rattles within my prison walls.

"In here," I yell, "Help me!"

Suddenly an old wooden ladder falls haphazardly into the well, I dodge left. Above I hear the music of hysterical laughter. Patsy. Seconds later, her full-faced smile is peering down at me from the top. "I would have been here sooner," she says, "but I didn't want the boys to catch me with the ladder. They would have tried to take it and I would have had to hurt them. Come on. Hurry up!"

I work to center the ladder against the wall, and begin my ascent; the old rungs creak with age. As I near the top, Patsy holds out her hand, "Next time you decide to take on those boys," she snickers, "you better wait for me." I nod, stretching out safely face down in the grass, hindsight is twenty-twenty.

"Sammie," Patsy says, with a snicker.

"Yes?"

"There's a feather sticking out of your butt," she giggles.

"Oh," I stretch back to look, emotionally worn, "Can you just pull it out for me?"

"Sure," she answers. I rest my face back into the grass.

Chapter Fifteen

Each day on the way home from school, Pearl and I pass by the Soda Shop. Today she does something a little different. She stops out front. "Sammie, come here, honey. Take these two nickels and run inside there to get us an ice cream."

She places the two nickels into my palm and I turn to walk toward the store. When I notice she isn't following behind me I turn around, "Aren't you coming in?"

"No, child, I ain't going in there."

"Well, how do I know what kind of ice cream you want?" I ask.

"I'm going to tell you. Vanilla, and we done been through this before. There are some places I just don't feel comfortable going into and that right there is one of them. I'll just wait right here on this little bench and you can bring it to me. No harm in that. Then we'll have a nice walk home, just you and me, eating our ice cream. Oh, get some napkins."

"Okay, I'll be right back." I stand on my tip-toes to tug open the heavy Soda Shop door. Once inside I see the long red counter with a soda jerk working on the other side in a black and white striped shirt and pointed hat.

"Can I help you," he asks.

"Yes, one small chocolate and one small vanilla ice cream cone."

He picks up a scoop and reaches down into a barrel of ice cream. Half inside the barrel, he peers up at me and asks, "Who's the other ice cream for?"

"My friend," I answer.

"Well, where's your friend?" he inquires, seems friendly enough.

I stare at him blankly, and automatically begin to shift my weight from one foot to the other, anxious to leave. This conversation mirrors a thousand others: "Why does that black lady walk you to school every day?" classmates ask, laughing among themselves. "Oh, is that your maid?" others ask, snidely with their friends. Mother says those people are small-minded. I agree. But I would prefer they disappear.

The "jerk" breaks my train of thought, "Well?" he questions. I tell myself that he means no harm, just making polite conversation, to calm down. "My friend," I answer, "is outside."

He stands up to peer through the window. "Is that black woman on the bench out there, that your friend?" he asks, apparently entertained by my awkwardness.

I feel the hair on my arms rise as I prepare for another battle, "Yes, it is," I snap.

"Whoa, touchy, touchy," he says, "I was just curious." He reaches over the separating glass to hand me the two cones. I quickly turn to leave with both hands full.

I have just placed my back against the heavy door preparing to push it open when the soda jerk calls out, "Hey!" I stop to look back. "Be sure to tell Miss Pearl I said hi. She's a real nice lady," he smiles.

I feeling rather foolish, return his smile and answer, "Thanks, yes, she is."

—∞—

Cleared of the door, ice cream cones in hand, I approach Pearl. "Oh, Lordy, ice cream," she says, reaching out for a cone. *"Whew,"* she says, "I've wanted one of their ice cream cones for a long, long time!" I do not reply. "What's the matter with you?" she says, her mouth full.

"Nothing. Just that soda jerk in there told me to tell you 'hi' is all."

"So," she says, "What's wrong with that? Why you mad?"

"I'm not mad," I sigh, "I just ALMOST got mad. And he's really cute. What's his name?"

"Andy. You went and got yourself all worked up, didn't you? And, he's too old for you."

"No. Well," I admit, "I almost got mad, but didn't. How old?"

Pearl smiles, "He's way too old for you! And good girl, I'm real proud of you. You got to pick your battles. I know that you mean well, but half the time there ain't nothing to it, really. You just get all worked up over something you can't do nothing about. BUT," she cocks her head, "on the other hand, it looks like we might be making some progress. Yes, it does." I swoon looking back toward the soda shop. "Oh, Lord," Pearl says, "Quick, hand me a napkin, I done made a mess."

Chapter Sixteen

It is Friday, and Patsy is coming to spend the night. We are walking home from school, indirectly, because I have ventured off of my normal path. We are actually several streets over.

As we walk along, our interest is drawn to a field filled with several piles of leaves. Each pile just begs to be jumped in. The only separation between us and paradise is one barbed wire fence which poses little obstacle. Once inside, I give Patsy a boost up into a shadowing tree, then follow. We each drop with delight down into the dry leaves.

Once each pile is duly flattened, with the leaves strewn hither and yon, we turn toward home. "You hear that?" I ask Patsy. "Hear what?" she answers, picking a twig from her dress. I turn to look behind us and in the distance, not far enough away, I see Mr. Ewell, the property owner, storming in our direction. His comb-over hair style is blowing in the wind, and his eyes are filled with rage. His baggy coveralls are held on by one strap, while the other slaps loosely in the breeze. In his hand he's swinging a heavy metal garden rake. He may be old, but he's not slow.

Swinging the rake high into the air, he yells, "You little rascals! Get out of my leaves!"

I turn to Patsy, "Come on. Let's get out of here!"

"Oh, Sammie!" Patsy yells. We take off running. In the rush I feel one of my brand new school shoes, a shiny black loafer slide off my foot. I don't dare stop to reach for it. We run toward the barbed wire fence and wrestle our way out. As I clear, I hear the unmistakable sound of material ripping as my dress catches on a barb. I still don't slow down. I am in a race with death.

I have only one remaining hurdle, a ditch, which I take like an Olympic athlete. I touch down nicely on the asphalt and turn to glance back, but I don't see Patsy. I am glad, however, to see that Mr. Ewell is blocked on the other side of the fence. "Patsy," I yell, scanning for her behind me. "Run!"

"I am running!" she answers. In spite of her weight, she is way ahead of me.

I glance back once more to see that Mr. Ewell is still on the other side of the fence. A few seconds later, his rake lands beside me, just a few feet off to my right side. We are homeward bound and in a hurry.

Once at home I dread the arrival of Mr. Ewell. I feel certain he will come to our house to tell my parents what we did. But maybe, we had been moving at such a rapid pace, such a speeding blur, that he hadn't seen who we were.

Soon the sun will set and Mr. Ewell has not arrived.

Patsy and I are both stretched out on the floor, watching *Rawhide* on television, when Mom, out of the blue, says "Sammie, why don't you bring your new school shoes out here to your father? So he can polish yours while he's doing his?" I roll my eyes at Patsy who has turned her head, trying to deflate a case of the giggles.

"Sammie, did you hear me?" Mom quizzes.

"Yes, ma'am," I acknowledge. I briefly consider bringing Dad my old black shoes, thinking he won't know the difference. But, I know Mom will. I decide to be honest. "Mom, I hate to tell you this, but I lost one of my shoes over in old man Ewell's yard."

"Samantha Lee! How many times have I told you to stay out of that hateful old man's yard?" Mom sighs and looks over at Dad for support. He is ignoring her.

"Sammie, we can't afford to buy you new shoes right now."

"I know, sorry," I acknowledge.

"So," she continues, "You'll either have to go back after dusk to try and find your shoe." Now Dad looks up, his eyebrows raised high. "Or," she continues, "You'll have to wear your old ones with the hole in the sole." Patsy and I share a dreadful glance. "Which is it?"

"I guess I don't have much choice. I'll go back tonight and try to find it."

"But Mama," Dad attempts to interrupt.

"Nope, don't you say anything," she responds, "Time she learns a lesson." Mom returns her focus to the television set while Dad looks over at me and shrugs.

Just after dusk, Patsy and I leave the safety of my home. Outside, as we leave, Dad is standing on the sidewalk. He appears to have been pacing its length in worry. As we pass by him, I nod. "Good luck," he says, "I'll be waiting right here. If you scream I'll hear you."

"Great, thanks, Dad, for your support," I answer, sarcastically.

Patsy and I slither back through the dark neighborhood relying on two old and dim streetlamps to guide our way. By the time we reach the barb-wired fence, we are holding hands, terrified. I stand on the bottom strand of wire and pull up on another. "Go on," I say to Patsy.

"Oh, no, you don't," she says, "you go first." She instead places her foot on the bottom wire, replacing mine. I ease through. "Now you come." We repeat the process in reverse.

"Man," I whisper, "If he's in here, I can't hear him." Patsy nods. Hand-in-hand, we circle each newly gathered pile of leaves. "Dang, I don't see it," I say to Patsy. She nods again. We move to a pile nearest the location where I believe I was when I lost it. "Okay," I mouth, "on the count of three, we're each going to stick a hand into that pile." I raise my fingers, one; two; three. In we thrust our hands; out they come, empty.

"Did you feel it in there?" I ask.

"No." Patsy shakes her head. "Forget it, Sammie, let's leave," she says, terrified. It was right about then that an apple fell from the tree causing both of us to about jump out of our skin. The grass under our feet flies as we take off running. We got out a lost faster than we got in.

I am relieved to have survived Mr. Ewell once more. I just hope I can survive my mother.

Saturday morning, I walk into the kitchen where Pearl is sweeping the floor.

"Morning, Pearl," I say as I reach past her for a couple homemade biscuits and hand one to Patsy.

"Morning," she looks up and rests the broom against the wall. "How'd it go last night? You find your shoe?"

"Nope," I say between chews. "We walked back over there after dark, but didn't find it."

"Uh-huh, I bet you looked real long and hard, too, didn't you?"

I smirk, "Of course, we looked real hard. But, truthfully, Pearl, it was like looking for a needle in a haystack. The whole time we were afraid that old man would hear us rustling around out there and grab his rake." I bite into my biscuit. "Pearl, do you think I ought to go back and look one more time?"

"Lord, child, don't talk with your mouth full! It's disgusting! And no!" she turns around, knocking the broom to the floor. "I don't want you going there ever again! I was worried, plum-to-death, last night. I lie in my bed just praying you all was all right. I couldn't even close my eyes. I hate to think about it." She shivers.

"You don't need to worry about me. I'm not stupid."

"Yes, you're a regular Einstein. If you were as smart as you apparently think you are, you never would have gone in there in the first place. Trespassing and all."

"I know, Pearl. You're right. You win."

"Well, I'll be. Finally." she nods, triumphantly, "I win. *Um, um.* I knew if I could just keep it up, that one day I would surely get lucky, and finally, today, sure enough, I win." She bends to pick the broom up from the floor.

Patsy gives me a confused look. "Welcome to my world," I say, shaking my head, "Always something."

1959

Chapter Seventeen

I am nine years old. I have progressed to a new stage, gangly and painfully thin. A string of freckles now run across the bridge of my nose and beneath the eye-catching pair of bright blue glasses my father picked out. If you've ever seen the television ad asking that you donate to support the starving children of the Appalachian Mountains, I could be that little girl, front and center.

I am one of those girls that plays tackle football with the boys. I am not afraid to get dirty and won't comb my hair until puberty. This past Christmas I received two contradictory gifts: a pair of cotton gloves for Cotillion, and a football helmet with a kicking tee.

―⚬―

I arrive home from school and look down to note that the zipper of my skirt, which should be in the back, is now in the front, and my knee socks are both down around my ankles in spite of the rubber bands. I am horribly thin. Weight will not stick to these bones.

As I walk past the mirror hanging in the living room I note that my hair, which is naturally curly, is way out of control. I appear to have two devil-like horns protruding from the sides of my head, so I fruitlessly try to smooth them down with spit.

"What in the world are you trying to do?" Pearl asks as she passes through the room.

I turn around, "I'm just ugly, look at me." I hold both arms out to my side. "I look like Olive Oyl from the Popeye cartoons. Not a bend or a curve. Straight, up and down."

"Ah, Honey, you ain't ugly," she says sympathetically as she folds some clothes.

"Pearl, come on," I challenge, "I know ugly when I see it. And, I would say, this is pretty much a good example."

"Looks don't matter," she corrects, "it's all about your heart."

"That's what everyone says to ugly people. How am I ever going to get a boyfriend?"

"You don't need be worrying about no boyfriend. You are too young for one thing, and too smart for the other."

"And I have a great personality." I slap my hands against my legs in frustration.

"Now, Miss Sammie," Pearl snaps, "Don't you make fun. There's something to be said for a great personality." I feel my eyes fill with desperate tears.

"My Mom is so beautiful, but look at me. What happened here? Maybe I'm adopted?" I head to the drawer where my parents hide their legal documents.

"Oh, Lord. You ain't adopted. Look. It seems to me that everybody is ugly once in their life. Either an ugly child or an ugly adult, but most everybody gets a case of the uglies sometime. Just think, if you're an ugly adult it lasts a whole lot longer, fifty, maybe even sixty years. But an ugly child always has the hope that someday they will grow out of it. Sure enough, most do. Well, of course, there's always an exception," she snickers."

"Like?" I inquire.

"Like what?"

"An exception. Give me one,"

"Okay, if it'll make you feel better. Miss Littmier. *Whew*, honey, that lady ain't never had a good day!" she shakes, "*Whew*."

"Pearl," I reprimand.

"Sorry," she answers, laughing.

I turn and head to my bedroom.

"Now hold on. Just hold on one second. I ain't done," she rushes up behind me.

"Your aunt. There you go. Your aunt. You think she's beautiful?"

"Yes, don't you?"

"That ain't the point. I remember her crying all the time. Tears rolling down her face because she thought she was so ugly."

"Was she?"

"Yes! She was pretty ugly, but that ain't the point either. The point is that when she hit sixteen she blossomed into a real beauty. Just when I think she couldn't get no prettier, she did. Plus, she has a kind heart.

"I never knew she was ugly," I respond.

"*Whew*!" She was. Anyway, now she's pretty, and she's your blood. Matter of fact, you favor her some. I bet you're going to blossom just like she did. I bet you're going put her pretty to shame. Yes'm. I bet you is." She turns to stare into my face. "And, you're kind like her. That will only make you prettier."

"Pearl, kind doesn't make you pretty."

"Well, MEAN can sure make people ugly!" she exclaims, "Like look at . . ."

"Pearl, don't. I get the point." She laughs again and shuffles off with an armful of dirty laundry.

I can feel my heart swell as Pearl leaves the room. She gives me hope. I don't know whether to laugh or cry. Search though I may I cannot find the written words to express how she makes me feel. I don't know. It's how you feel, if you can imagine, when someone has devoted her entire life and breath to improve your life. When someone insists that you are going to do something magnificent one day, and every single normal day they swear you already have. It's when someone loves you so unselfishly that their every dream, prayer and success is achieved when you return through the door unharmed. She, who has little, gives me all she has—her time and her vision.

"Pearl," I yell through the house.

"Yes'm," her voice echoes from the kitchen.

"I just want to tell you that . . . I . . . THINK . . . YOU . . . ARE . . . GORGEOUS!"

"Yes'm," she snickers, "I am. I sure am. Least I know them glasses you got on work."

1960

Chapter Eighteen

Another school day finished. I have just cleared the doorway and am grateful to see the sunshine, when a friend, a boy, approaches and asks if I will cover for him as school crossing guard tomorrow morning. I agree, and he hands me his patrol belt and badge. I am excited about doing something new and glad to help out my friend.

The next morning, I leave the house a few minutes early and take my post on the appropriate corner. While I am directing the younger children across the street, I see the school principal approaching. When he reaches me he asks me to step aside. He proceeds to inform me that I am not permitted to serve as a crossing guard because . . . well, I am a girl. His logic seems to imply that because I am a girl, I cannot adequately meet the responsibilities of the charge. I have never been told that I am in any way limited due to my sex. I've heard about people who make that absurd claim, but it has never happened to me. I hand him my gear and head toward the school.

Pearl is surprised when I arrive home a little early. She had allotted additional time for my new assignment. "Oh, you're early," she says.

"Yes, Mr. Benton said I couldn't be a crossing guard."

"Why not?" she asks, crumbling her apron in her hands.

"Because I'm a girl."

"Oh, Lord a mercy," she says, disapprovingly, but returns to her dusting.

"Anyway, that's that." I am not so disappointed about losing the position, as I am by the insinuation I am incapable. I throw myself down on the couch and try to hide a serious attitude.

"Oh, Miss Sammie," Pearl says, dust rag resting on her hip, "You just got to shake that off. He's just a foolish man, doing what's been done for a long time. Not likely to change anytime soon." She moves to sit beside me on the couch.

"Well, it makes me want to cuss a blue streak," I mumble, my arms folded across my chest in disgust.

"Well, I definitely wouldn't be doing that, Miss Sammie. Your Mama will have a bar of soap in your mouth before you get the first two words out. You remember the last time you tried that? You were sick for days," she reminds.

"Uh-huh, I remember."

"Yeah, me too," she snorts. "You remember, neither one of us could leave the house. You sick, and me just a watching." I fall into her lap, giggling.

―⁓―

We are settled in for a quiet night of television when the phone rings, and Mom moves across the room to answer it. Dad is resting in his chair, his feet up on the hassock, recovering from a long commute. I hear Mom hang up the phone, and soon she steps into the living room. "That was Mrs. Archer. She said that Will cannot be at his school guard crossing post tomorrow and wanted to know if Sammie could fill in for him again? Guess she doesn't know what happened. I didn't tell her. I said I'd call her back."

Before her statement registers in my brain, Dad perks up in his chair. "Go call her back. Tell her Sammie will be there."

"Dad," I try to reason, "Have you lost your mind? Sometimes I think you try to get me into trouble. I don't care that much, really. Let's just forget about the whole thing." But he is adamant, so Mom calls Mrs. Archer back and tells her I'll be there in the morning.

Dad drives me to my assigned corner and pulls over to let me out. I watch as he pulls away, apparently on his way to work. I have no belt or badge to identify my position since it was confiscated yesterday, but I move to take my post. As I am waiting on the curb I believe I see something out of the corner of my eye, behind the hedge. I can't check it out because a group of children is waiting to cross, so I step into position. I occasionally glance back in that direction, but try to remain focused on the job at hand.

Shortly, as expected, I see the principal walking down the street in my direction. This time, though, he looks angry. He is moving so quickly that his coat is blown open in his breeze. I accept that my stint is over and prepare to be informed.

Waiting impatiently on the other side of the street is another crowd of children. I step down to the median and wave for them to cross.

When I return my gaze to the principal, he still has not reached my position. Along the way he has been intercepted. I squint to see a man clumsily pushing his way through the hedge. My Dad. He looks ridiculous as he fights off the attacking bushes. I shake my head in disbelief.

I stand near the crossing, just waiting for someone to give me the word. Stay or go. It appears their discussion is over. They are shaking hands. The principal is turning back toward the school, and Dad is once again tied up in the bushes. Just as he clears an escape route, and lifts one foot to step through the hedge, he glances up, his bright smile, "Guess I got him straightened out," he says, and steps out of sight.

"Yes, Dad, of course, you did," I whisper, "I'm sure you did."

In my family, we, the children, are not allowed to use the word "can't." The girls are expected to be as physical and hearty as the boys.

It is an early summer morning, my uncle and I have just arrived at the river, we are going fishing. As we near our favorite spot, an abandoned dock we discovered last summer, he pulls off the side of the road and tells me to go ahead and get out. I stand nearby, watching as he pulls off into a clearing in the woods. The old truck leans heavily left, then right, nearly tipping over, but fighting its way through the weeds and bumps. Finally, it comes to rest at the foot of an old oak tree. My uncle, soon recognizing that his door is blocked by the tree, scoots over the passenger's side and climbs out. "Guess I didn't do that very well," he laughs. He saunters back to the truck bed and reaches in for our fishing gear, "Here, gal," he says, handing me the poles and bait. "You go on ahead," he instructs, "Watch out for those prickers." Thankfully, I have worn my long pants. Years of fishing experience has already taught me that the burrs and thorns here are merciless.

Arriving at the dock, I stop to appreciate the sounds, the smells and the fog that still rests on the river's reflective surface. I bend to set down my gear and return my focus to the awe of nature. As I stand lost in the glory of spending some quiet time alone with my uncle, he, who has the evasive skills of an Indian warrior, sneaks up behind me and throws me into the dark murky water. When I bob up to the surface he is already yelling, "Now swim to the other side!"

"I really wish you wouldn't do that!" my voice carries through the fog. "Seems the 'least you could do is give me some kind of warning! And, I can't. It's too far! Plus, I still have my shoes on!" I yell, treading water.

"What was that that just came out of your mouth?" he asks, hands on his hips. "It wasn't the words 'I can't' was it?

"No, I said I still have my shoes on!" At that point I reach down and slide my feet out of my shoes and swim over to place them on the dock by his feet.

"Well, Gal, now suppose," he says, looking down at me, "Just suppose you were on a ship in the ocean and it sank. What would you do then, just whine and yell *'I can't'* and drown? He squeals and wiggles imitating a little girl. By God, you can do it and you will. So just get moving. Two laps, over and back! I'll be waiting right here." My uncle is, by his very nature, a teacher. I instinctively accept the fact that everything he does is to introduce a lesson he deems important. As I swim across, I try to figure out just what that lesson might be.

Midday, I come dragging into the house. My pants are filthy and my shoes are soaked with so much water that they squeak. I bend down to shed them by the front door.

Pearl comes around the corner, "Now, what happened to those shoes? You people act like you made of money or something," she says shaking her head in disapproval.

Pulling off a soaked sock, I say, "Well, somehow I ended up in the river with my shoes still on my feet."

"That man, I swear. I think he crazy as a loon. His Mama must have dropped him on his head or something," she says, handing me an old towel.

"Yes, well," I respond, "I can't do anything about it. He's mine."

"Yes, it's not your fault. Only God can love that man." Socks off, I bend down to pick them up.

"Now just where you think you're going to put those nasty old things?" she asks, exasperated.

"In the laundry basket," I tease.

"Oh, no, you ain't!" she says, slapping my behind and confiscating the socks.

Chapter Nineteen

I am seated midway in class, the fourth grade, trying not to draw any attention. Patsy sits at the desk across the aisle. I have, for the ump-teenth time, failed the time-telling test. The teacher has mandated that pupils who don't pass the test get no recess. No recess again today. It's been approximately two months since I've had recess. The only thing that makes it bearable is that Patsy stays inside to keep me company. My parents are unaware of my current school challenge because, as a rule, students are not permitted to blame their own failures on their teachers, so I don't. Also, it's a matter of pride to have no issues with your teachers, especially when most of the women in our family are teachers. I just keep hoping that someday this year, I may pass.

Recess completed, the other children are back inside and class is again in session when I see Samson staring through the classroom window. He's jumping up and down, tail wagging, whining a little. I try to ignore him, hoping he will go home.

"Whose dog is that?" says the teacher with her eyes scanning the room for a held up hand.

"Mine," I say, hand in the air.

"Well, if that dog doesn't leave here right now I am going to call the pound to come get it!"

"Yes, ma'am," I acknowledge.

When I get a chance, I pass a note to Patsy. It reads, "I am leaving to take my dog home. If they call my parents to come in, tell them what happened." She looks at me with an "Oh, you're not" look, but I nod that, yes, I am leaving. She drops her head heavily to the desk.

"Mrs. Rogers?" I say.

"Yes Sammie?"

"I have to go to the bathroom."

"I'm sure you can wait."

"No, Ma'am, actually I can't." I jiggle around for effect. Patsy's giggle kicks in, but I cut my eyes at her to stop, immediately.

"Okay, go on," Mrs. Rogers says. I look over at Patsy and nod. Again her head hits the desk.

I try to restrain my emotions as I walk slowly out of classroom and turn right toward the Exit door. Once out of sight, I hit that door flying, and call for my dog, who quickly appears at my side. Together, we head for home.

As I come running into the house, I have to swerve to avoid Pearl. "Lord a mercy Girl!" she squeals, "What you running from? The police or something?"

"Maybe," I answer and walk directly to my bedroom where I close the door, my dog inside. From the other side of the door I hear Pearl, *"Um, um, um.* What has that child gone and done now?"

It's late in the evening and no one has mentioned the school/dog event. I think perhaps I am home free. But no, my father patiently broaches the subject. "Sammie, did you miss school today?" I cringe.

"Not exactly, sir."

"What do you mean by 'not exactly'?" The tears begin to roll down my face as I apologize to my father because I cannot pass the time-telling test. I tell him how I've stayed inside during recess for several months because I'm so stupid. How thankful I am that Patsy always stayed inside with me. Lastly, I divulge how the teacher's threat to have Samson taken to the pound was more than I could handle. "I'm sorry, Daddy," I say, and prepare for the worst, no television.

Dad rises from his chair and walks over to me. He rests his heavy hand on my shoulder. "Its okay, Sammie," he says. "I'll see what I can do to help, okay?" I nod my head, yes.

—⁂—

The next day I return to class, expecting to get a severe tongue lashing from the teacher or be told to go to the Principal's Office. I am waiting, when a voice comes over the classroom speaker. "Mrs. Rogers, will you come to the office for a moment please?"

"Of course," she answers, smiling as if she's won the Teacher of the Year Award. Before she leaves the room, she stops to give us instructions. Holding her hands up shoulder high, palms down, she instructs, "We will stay in our seats like little ladies and gentlemen until I get back." She closes the door behind her.

Immediately, Patsy leans over to whisper, "Sammie, I heard my Daddy talking to your Daddy last night. Something's going on."

"They're probably mad at me."

"No, Sammie, I don't think so," she consoles. "I bet you a quarter the family is waiting for Ms. Rogers in the Office." I feel sick to my stomach. Now I've done it. I suddenly feel sorry for Ms. Rogers.

We wait for what seems like an eternity, me glancing over at Patsy, she glancing over at me. Nods and shrugs. Finally, a different teacher walks into the classroom. "Boys and girls, I will be your substitute for the next few days until they find a replacement for Ms. Rogers," she announces. I look over to see that Patsy has extended her thumb upward. She smiles and mouths, "Told you."

I rest my head and arms on the desk. I am neither happy, nor sad. Poor Ms. Rogers, I think, wish I could say that I'll miss you.

I would later discover that an emergency family meeting had been called and the decision was unanimous: Mrs. Rogers needs to go. She will never return to our classroom.

Chapter Twenty

****

- *CBS Evening News* with Douglas Edwards: Today, February 1, 1960. Four African American college students were charged with trespassing after they entered a Woolworth's in Greensboro, North Carolina and requested service at the whites-only counter. When the clerk refused service and asked them to leave the premises they expressed their objection by remaining in their seats.

****

I open my eyes to find an early spring morning. The bedroom curtains are dancing in the breeze of an open window. It is one of those remarkably beautiful days. The kind of day you know you will always remember about home. Better yet, it's Saturday. I lay soothingly cocooned in the goose-down comforter sewn by my maternal grandmother. I take a moment to enjoy the peace and quiet.

Just outside my bedroom door I hear a, *crash!* "Ooops," Pearl whispers as she turns to make sure she has not disturbed my sleep.

"Hi, Pearl, I'm awake."

"Sorry, I was trying to be quiet," she says.

"Pearl, I don't think that being quiet is one of your gifts."

"Reckon not," she answers, returning to her work.

I dig my way out from under the warmth of the feathers and steady myself on the side of the bed. I hate putting my feet on the over-waxed wooden floor. The layers have become sticky and clammy. It's like walking on glue. I search around, to find my bunny slippers nearby. I stretch my legs out to nudge them closer. Done, I stand and wedge my feet deep into the fat slippers, reaching down to push the bunny ears off to the side.

"Yes, you best watch them bunny ears," Pearl says, "They going to trip you up." I don't respond, I just smile, appreciating her concern.

Feet finally on the floor, I head out through the doorway walking like a bow-legged cowboy. The bunny ears have returned to their proper bunny position, making each about nine inches wide.

"Sammie," mother says, from the living room chair. I shrink. She has apparently been waiting for me to get up. Typically, that's not good news for me. I stand in place in the hallway, afraid to step into the lion's den. "Sammie," she says, again.

"Yes, Mom?" I relent and answer, still in the hallway, rolling my eyes at Pearl.

"I've been thinking." Those words alone send a feeling of doom down my spine. I remain still and glance over at Pearl. She whispers, "Oh, Lord. Missus, been thinking again." I cut her my 'you're so funny' look as I step into mother's view.

"I think it's time for you to start taking piano lessons," Mom shares.

I throw my head back in utter desperation. "But, Mom," I say, now recovering from my self-inflicted whiplash.

"Nope," she interrupts.

"Mom, I was just going to ask, if it is a state law or something that girls have to take piano lessons? Where's Dad?"

"At the barber shop. And, no, Sam, it's not a law, but you will thank me later. Who knows, you may even enjoy it, God forbid."

"Mom, you know I hate that kind of stuff." I move nearer to her, minding my bunnies. "Suppose I said I don't want to? Would that make any difference to you?"

She closes her magazine, taking her sweet time before she answers, "Too bad, you begin Monday after school. Good morning! Come over here and give me a hug. I'll tell you where your classes are."

"Oh, Mom," I say, wretched with despair.

I am about a month into my piano lessons. When I arrive my piano teacher is sitting outside in her sunroom. She weighs no less than three hundred pounds, and other students have told me that she uses her size to intimidate them. I walk over to the piano stool and plop myself down. She peels herself from a metal rocking chair and moves to the piano bench, beside me. I feel the bench groan from her weight.

"Did you practice your keys last night?" she asks.

"No, ma'am, I didn't. I practiced my English on a cue-ball."

"Sammie, if you do not practice nightly, you will not be successful. And I may be forced to sit on you," she laughs good-naturedly. "How would you like that?"

"Not so much," I respond, "but I doubt I would be able to complain about it. If you do, sit on me that is, please make it fast. Don't make me suffer too long." She smiles, apparently appreciating my sarcasm.

"Okay, start playing your keys," she prompts.

—∞—

The part I particularly dislike about taking piano lessons is my required participation in yearly recitals. Mother says I suffer from stage fright.

"Please, Mama, I'd rather take a beating than go to another recital," I beg. I see my brother laughing as I am tortured and give him my, 'I'll get you later, look.'

"Oh, Sammie, don't be so dramatic," Mom says, with not a lick of sympathy. "Now go get ready. You have to be on-stage in forty-five minutes!"

—∞—

My mother waits with me backstage. "Oh, Sammie, you look so cute!" she sighs.

"Mom, this dang crinoline is killing me. Why don't you just use a guillotine if you're trying to punish me or something."

Earnestly, she bends down and peers into my eyes, "Just remember, Sam, do your best. We will be proud of you either way, good or bad. Good luck!" she says spritely, exiting to join the other proud parents waiting in the auditorium.

Year after year, armed only by the grace of God, do I manage to scrape through my memorized musical piece. And, immediately upon its conclusion, I begin to dread the next.

―⚘―

The torture and humiliation of piano lessons do, in fact, present an opportunity. The teacher has planned a trip to New York City for her students. We will ride a bus from Virginia. I would never admit it, but I am excited to ride an elevator, see the Empire State Building and the Statue of Liberty.

―⚘―

I bound down from the bus, glad to be home. I was homesick before I left.

"Pearl, I'm home!" I yell.

She comes rushing around the corner, delighted, "Oh, Miss Sammie, I'm so glad to see you. It's been way too quiet around here. How was your trip? Tell me everything!" She sits down on the couch, poised to listen.

"It was good. We went to a ballet, and the theatre. I got stuck in the elevator. It was great. Oh," I reach down to retrieve a little white bag from my suitcase, "I bought you something," and hand it to her.

She reaches out, gently taking the bag, but she doesn't move to open it. I wait a few seconds before encouraging her, "Pearl, aren't you going to open it?"

She raises her head a little, "Yes. Of course, I will. I'm just really touched that you'd think of Pearl when you was in New York City. And then you even bring me a gift and all."

"Of course, I would bring you something, Pearl. Open it!"

I watch as her wrinkled fingers fumble to open the bag. Finally, she reaches the tissue paper and delicately unfolds it to reveal a plastic key chain. A replica of the Empire State Building hangs from it.

"Miss Sammie. Ain't that beautiful?" she says in delight, holding it high into the air. "I got me a key chain all the way from New York City."

"Like it?" I ask, always needing her confirmation.

"Yes'm, I sure do." She cradles the charm in her hands, studying it. "Thank you, Miss Sammie. Thank you so much. Pearl is so lucky to have you care about her." She looks over in my direction, awaiting an appropriate response.

"Me, too," I say.

"Me too, what?" she smiles, knowing my difficulty with expressing feelings.

"Me, too, I'm lucky to have you, Pearl," I struggle to complete. Embarrassed, by the display of affection, I grab my suitcase and retreat to my bedroom. In the background I hear her cackle.

"It ain't funny," I say, still in motion.

"Is too," she answers.

1961

- *CBS Radio Network, Howard K. Smith* reporting: Today, May 14, 1961, Mother's Day, I, responding to a tip, was on the scene to witness a vicious mob of Klansmen as they attacked a group of Freedom Riders at the Birmingham *Trailways Bus* Station. The Freedom Riders group is comprised of student volunteers, both black and white. They have been traveling through Alabama testing the recent Supreme Court order that outlaws segregation in interstate travel facilities.

While my social life at school appears to be improving, I am contending with some fairly severe issues at home. I have been very distracted by an obvious change in my father. I find it to be quite unsettling. The "in-house privacy law" demands that I keep personal problems to myself, so I try to function at school as though things are normal. It is difficult at best, and my stress sometimes presents itself as anger and frustration.

My father, a World War II veteran, is having flashbacks of events, terrifying events. His sleeping habits are fluctuating and his eating habits are poor. It appears the demons of his past are overtaking him, and the apparent result is sweet to horrifying mood swings with occasional hallucinations. During these mood swings, his personality morphs in and out of his alternate personality which is particularly confrontational.

I appear to be the only one who can bring him any comfort during these transformations. I can only suppose it's because he does not perceive me as a threat. My interludes with this stranger, who happens to resemble my father, will fluctuate over the next ten years. By the time my assignment is completed, I should easily qualify as a hostage negotiator.

****
- *CBS News Report*—1961—Howard K. Smith resigns from CBS and moves to ABC following a dispute with executives over a documentary he produced, "*Who Speaks for Birmingham?*"

****

Tonight I am laying in bed, somewhere between awake and asleep, buried deep under the covers with my arm over my trusted old dog. I hear the door to my room open and feel the end of my bed sink from my father's weight. He sits on my toes. His shadowed form appears to be hunched forward with his head resting heavily in his hands. I lie very still, playing possum, in a feeble attempt to avoid another altercation. I feel my bed jiggle, kind of like one of the motel "magic finger" beds, so I slightly angle my head so I can see him. I watch as he raises his arm to wipe his face. It hits me hard—my father is crying. My eyes automatically begin to fill, my nose tickles as it prepares to run, and my heart sinks to a desperate place. I focus on his each and every mumbled word.

"Sammie," he says, "I don't want you to be ashamed of me, but I've seen some horrible things. Things no one should ever have to see. I can't get them out of my head. I try." I strain to lie still. "Daddy," he continues, "cannot tell anyone but you, Sam. I know you will love me anyway." He has my full attention.

"Sammie, Daddy stood by and watched as a seventeen-year-old boy was blown to bits. He was too young to be in the War so I was trying to get him to back safety. He hadn't even graduated from high school. Our parameter was enclosed by landmines. I drove him through the course once to show him the layout. But when he tried it on his own, he hit . . ." Dad stops to cry. "I failed him," he says, gasping for air. I wait while he tries to regains his composure. "This will have to be our secret, Sam," he whispers, and I flinch, "Just you and me, Sam, our little secret." I feel his weight lift from the bed. "Sleep tight," he says, closing the door behind him.

Now I am in a predicament. He thinks I am asleep so I can't discuss it with him. And because it is a secret, I can't discuss it with anyone else. For all the times he has stood by me, I feel obligated to try to help him. I just hope I can.

I spend many nights beside my Dad, and many days trying to talk him down as he once again points his index finger to the sky, pulls back his thumb, and shoots at the imaginary "Japs" flying over our house. I wait until he clears the sky. I have been down this road before. Once the threat has been annihilated, he will come inside where we can relax, safe and sound. It's just another day in anti-aircraft artillery.

As the months turn to years, my father desperately tries to overcome his nightmares of carnage. One minute he is vulnerable and begging us for understanding; the next, he is aggressive and clear that he needs no one, no one. Our reaction as a family is all about the visuals and the verbiage. People cannot process what they cannot imagine, try though they might. Our family is becoming yet another victim of the War. I, armed with a little more information than the others, am determined to ride this out and bring home my father.

Chapter Twenty-Two

Tonight, my mother arrives home from work, visibly shaken. I am perched on a stool in the kitchen watching Pearl put together a meatloaf casserole for dinner. I overhear Mom ask, "Honey, can you come talk to me a minute?"

"Of course," Dad answers.

Pearl and I can overhear bits of their conversation. It appears that another man, besides my father, is seeking mother's attention. She informs Dad that midway through the day "a male co-worker" cornered her in an office where she was filing documents.

It is at this point, Pearl and I turn to face each other wide-eyed. "Pearl . . . ," I say.

"*Shhhh,* child, I'm trying to listen."

My mother generally has little problem defending herself, verbally or physically, but as the conversation continues it becomes clear that there are other considerations at play. While she did manage to escape unscathed, she still faces the possibility that she may be assaulted again, which leads her to believe she should approach management for intervention. On the other hand, she is concerned, should she approach management and complain about a favored male employee, they may retaliate against her. Another consideration she brings to the forefront is the likelihood the event will attract community gossip. Pearl and I are still leaning toward the kitchen door, focused in on the conversation.

I peek around the corner to see that Mom and Dad are sitting together on the couch. He is holding her hands in his, listening. Nothing can unite our family like a good outside challenge. Dad sits, patiently listening to her recount the event, while she shares her contempt for the offender.

"That's it," mother says. "That's what happened." We hear no response from Dad. He is unusually tranquil. Generally, he would be pacing around the room, poised for a fight, but he appears sympathetic. Finally, he turns to her and whispers, "It's all right, honey, it's not your fault. I'll see what I can do."

"I appreciate it," she says. "Thank you so much for being so understanding." I watch as she leans in to kiss him, "But," she continues, "I want to try and handle this on my own. Okay? I will go in to work tomorrow and speak with the Manager. I don't want you to do anything. If I need your help, I'll let you know."

"All right, honey, if that's what you want me to do," he answers. "I respect that."

Pearl immediately throws herself back against the kitchen counter in shock. "Ah, he ain't going to do no such thing!" she says. "I just know he's going to do something!" She is practically circling the kitchen. "Either he's not telling," she continues, "or something's bad wrong with him. Uh-huh."

Once again, I peek into the living room to see Dad gently lift Mama's chin with his fingers. Love.

The next morning my mother is dressed in her red power suit and matching spiked heels. The ensemble itself sends a message: she means business.

Dad left for work hours earlier, as usual. Our day begins as any other.

Pearl and I stand by the door as mother leaves for work. Shortly, I will make my way to school as well. "Bye, Mama," I say, "Good luck." She leans down to kiss me. "Thanks, I'll need it," she smiles.

"Yes, Missus, you just give them what for," Pearl instructs.

Mom reaches out to hug Pearl, "Thanks, I will."

―⚉―

"I cannot believe you!" Mother yells behind her as she arrives home from work. "You sat right here and lied to my face!" Hearing the onset of a confrontation, Pearl and I rush back to the kitchen and take our eavesdropping positions.

"And here I was! I bought the whole thing, hook, line and sinker!" Mom continues. Dad steps inside the house.

"I said I'm sorry. What else can I say?" he asks.

"Not one damn thing! You have no defense."

"Don't cuss," Dad answers, "It's not becoming. Ladies don't cuss! You want the kids to cuss?"

"Don't even give me that. Brother already cusses like a sailor and last week I had to wash Sammie's mouth out with soap for the third time! And you! You act as if your going into my workplace and assaulting someone is proper behavior!" she responds. "You are beyond words.

It's like talking to a brick wall. I arrive at work and there you are. You not only scared the crap out of him, but everyone else in the place! Not to mention that you embarrassed me to death!"

"He needed the crap scared out of him. That S.O.B." Dad holds firm. "How many women you think he's done that to? Just you? You really think you're the only one? Answer me that! It's okay for him to go around scaring women? You want to unleash him on someone else? With him thinking he can keep it up and won't ever have to pay the piper? I'll tell you what. He's lucky I didn't shoot him. Mildred's husband would have just shot him, then there'd be no need for talking!" Dad huffs, plopping himself down heavily into his chair.

"Well," Mom answers, sarcastically, "that is probably the only true statement you've made so far. I am surprised you didn't shoot him. I wondered why you were acting so sensitive and caring and considerate . . . not normal!" Dad remains still in his chair, his head down. He knows only time will make her mellow.

"This is not the Wild West, shoot first and ask questions later," Mom continues. "Oh, hell, it's done," she wipes her hands together, looking over at Dad.

"I said don't cuss," he repeats.

"I didn't," she denies, "It's just a wonder you didn't get arrested."

"Dale isn't going to arrest me," he scoffs, "He's my best friend. That will never happen."

"I wouldn't press my luck on that," she warns, "One day, if you keep that up, he may have to. Like Pearl always says, 'things change.'" She storms from the room, spiked heels in hand.

J. M. Duke

Dad picks his feet up and rests them on the hammock. Unfazed, he yells out, "Pearl, you hear that all real good? Or do you want us to repeat it?"

Pearl's throws her hands to her face. I laugh out loud. Busted.

1962

Chapter Twenty-Three

"Your uncle dropped off some of his sweet corn for supper!" mother says, carrying a bowl to the dinner table.

We are just pulling out the chairs to sit down for dinner when the phone rings. Dad pulls his chair back from the table and turns to answer it. Usually the calls are for Mom, but, surprisingly not this time. The gist of the conversation I overhear is that Raymond, Pearl's brother, needs to borrow a couple hundred dollars.

I sit and listen attentively from the table as Dad speaks, "Sure, tell Ray I'll be there in a minute," he says, and hangs up.

"I have to go out," he says, turning to us, "but I'll be back real soon. Go ahead and eat supper without me." We sit and watch as he scurries about, gathering up his car keys and wallet. Soon he opens the front door and closes it behind him.

Hours later, Mom and I are still sitting in the living room, waiting either for the telephone to ring or Dad to return home. Mom, who is not best known for her patience, picks up the phone and dials Raymond's number. Remarkably, he answers. Confused, she asks, "Raymond, what are you doing at home?"

"What do you mean by 'what am I doing at home'? What's wrong Missus?"

"I thought you two were going to meet somewhere?" she says, her panic obvious.

"Who? Mister? Meet? Where?"

"I don't know. Someone called here. I assumed it was you. Anyway, they said you needed to borrow some money right away, so he rushed out to bring it to you."

"No, Ma'am," he says, "It wasn't me that called."

Mom reaches for the chair to sit down. "Oh, my God," she says.

"Missus, don't you worry now. I'm going to find out what's going on here. Edgar and I will leave right now to look for him. Don't you worry. I'll call you the minute we find him. Just stay in the house and wait for me to call. Okay?"

"Okay, Raymond, thank you," she whispers, resting the phone in its cradle.

—⚉—

Mom remains motionless for fifteen, maybe twenty minutes later, before the phone rings, breaking her trance.

"Raymond?" she answers.

"We found him, Missus. He was lying in the alley next to the church in town. They hurt him pretty bad so we carried him straight here to the hospital. His money was gone, Missus. Somebody took it, but left his wallet. I done called his Daddy, so he's already on the way to pick you up. I told him you weren't in no shape to be driving, being so upset and all."

"Thank you, Raymond. The kids and I will be waiting for him to arrive."

"Okay, Missus, we are going to be right here in the Emergency Room waiting for you."

When we arrive at the hospital, Raymond and Edgar are sitting off to the side in the Waiting Room. Hats in hand, they walk over to meet us. I climb up into Raymond's arms. Brother, keeping a good distance from Edgar, finds a chair to sit down.

"I'm sorry, Missus. I didn't have nothing to do with hurting him. He's my friend," Raymond confirms.

"I know that, Raymond. Don't be silly. That never even crossed my mind," she reaches up to pat his massive shoulder.

Across the room is a local police officer, writing a report.

Raymond leans to mother and whispers, "He," pointing to the officer, "seems to think that maybe we, me and Edgar, had something to do with it. He's been asking us all kinds of questions."

"Well, don't worry, Raymond. I'll speak to him." She walks directly over to the officer who looks up and stops writing.

"Officer," she points across the room, "Raymond is worried that you suspect him and his brother. I want to assure you that they cannot possibly be involved in this. They have both worked for our family for many years. In fact, it was Raymond and Edgar who went looking for him and carried him to the hospital."

"Yes, ma'am," he responds, "but doesn't that sound a little too convenient?"

"Convenient?" she bites. "They found my husband! I called Raymond's house and he was home!"

"Yes, ma'am, but we have to check everything."

My grandfather, attracted by my mother's apparent infuriation, strolls across the room. He stands nearby and listens for a few minutes before, apparently unimpressed, he interrupts, "Officer, don't you think it would be more beneficial if you focused on who assaulted my son? I mean any fool can take the shortest route by picking an easy target," he challenges. "Why, who knows," he emphasizes, "I bet, if you were to try real hard, that you may actually solve a crime. I mean, after all, that is what we, the taxpayers, pay you for." I see that his eyes are locked in on the officer. "Right now, son," he continues, "you're just wasting time." That said, he turns toward us, "Raymond, you and Edgar go on home. I'll call you tomorrow with any news. Thank you very much for all you've done."

"Yes sir," Raymond nods. He carries me over to my mother, shakes hands with grandfather and leaves. Edgar trails behind. As he passes, Brother meets his gaze apprehensively and sinks further into his chair.

Together, the four of us walk down the hallway searching for Dad's room. As we enter we see another police officer inside, asking questions. My uncle is propped up against the wall, apparently overseeing the situation. News of a family emergency spreads quickly.

My mother swoons as we enter. My father has tubes and bandages around his nose and down his throat. His right leg is suspended into the air by a brace that descends from the ceiling.

"Did you recognize your attackers?" the officer asks.

"No, I didn't. Damn, I already told you that. They had on masks and gloves! I can tell you it wasn't Raymond or Edgar. Could have been white, for all I know," Dad is noticeably perturbed as he struggles to get his elbows under him to sit up. "Whoever did this obviously set me up. They probably set up Raymond and Edgar too, to take the blame." He relents from the struggle and falls back into the pillows. "Whoever did this," he adds, "planned to rob me as soon as I arrived."

"Sir, your money..." the Officer begins to respond, but is interrupted by the entry of his superior, Sheriff Dale Wiggins.

"How you doing?" Dale asks, looking over at Dad.

"How do I look?" Dad answers, sarcastically.

"You look horrible. Got quite a shiner."

"Look Dale, I don't give a damn about the money," Dad informs his friend, "but you know, well as I do, that Raymond and Edgar didn't have anything to do with this. And I don't want anyone bothering them." He fights to free his leg from the brace.

"Slow down, who said they had something to do with it?" Dale asks.

"Him," Dad points directly at the officer who places his hands to his chest in a gesture of innocence.

"I got this," Dale says, turning to the officer, "You go on back to the scene. See if they left any clues. Speak to Mrs. Holman across the street, maybe she saw something. Don't bother anyone unnecessarily, including the two brothers. If need something from them you go through me. You hear?"

"Yes sir," the officer answers, now turning to leave. My uncle expedites his exit by opening the door.

"We'll find 'em," Dale says, turning back to Dad, "Got any ideas? You made anybody mad lately?"

"Nah," Dad smirks, "Least not on purpose."

"Well, I got a few ideas," my uncle says, motioning for my grandfather and Dale to step up to form a huddle.

"Dale," Dad teases, "You better not listen to those vigilantes. If I knew who it was or why it happened I would tell you. I can only tell you whoever called sounded black, but who knows. They claimed to be a friend of Raymond's, don't know that either. Guess someone needed the money pretty bad. Obviously, one thing they did know was that Raymond and I are friends. They hit me in my weak spot, I guess. Should have been more careful."

Dad eases back down into the fluff of a pillow and releases a heavy sigh. I watch as he reaches gently for mother and pulls her down close to his face, "You do know that you, Raymond and Edgar probably saved my life? I'm sorry, honey. The next time I won't go alone."

Mom looks at him with an easy smile, "I hope there's no next time."

"Oh, I hope there is a next time," my uncle says from across the room, "because the next time I'm going with you." His brown eyes are locked on my father, who nods. They have an unspoken code.

As I sit, curled up in one of the hospital chairs, Pearl crosses my mind. Particularly one of her sayings: "Sometimes child," she says, "trying to do the right thing hurts." Like my Dad trying to help Raymond. I wonder if Dad would go again. Sure, he would. I only hope that he asks my Uncle to go along next time.

"Sammie," I hear my father say, "Come here, Gal." My uncle steps up to lift me into the hospital bed.

I will never hear another word mentioned as to who or why someone would attack my father. Secrets run deep in our family, once they are either buried or rectified, they rarely resurface. I would feel fairly certain to say, that it is very unlikely that the perpetrators were not sought out and discovered, some time, by someone, in some place.

This weekend our family will have its annual family reunion. Relatives travel from all over the state to attend. Our city relatives will arrive in station wagons, the women wearing bright red lipstick. Our country relatives will arrive in pick-up trucks, the truck beds filled to the brim with freckled children.

It has been quite a few years since the confrontation between my Grandmother and me. I don't mention it, and neither does she, but we know. We speak to each other only on an "as needed" basis. I sometimes pine for an endearing and loving grandmother, but prefer no attention to the type of indifference I had been receiving. Pearl counsels that things will change someday. She says I need to "leave the door open" for healing and reconciliation. I must admit that I am not particularly overcome by grief.

Today I am at my grandparents' house, seated in the kitchen, running my fingers over the patterns of the red and white plaid tablecloth. The house and yard are bustling with activity as we prepare for our guests.

"Sammie," my grandmother says, grabbing my attention, "I would like for you to wash your hands and knead the bread dough for me please."

"Yes, ma'am," I answer, moving to the sink. She steps to the table, removes the tablecloth and dusts the top with flour. Again in place, my hands now clean, she places a large ball of dough on the table. I sink my hands deep into the gooey dough, push and pull, pull and push.

"Child," Pearl says, standing by the sink. "If your arms get tired just let me know. I'll call in Lila to take your place for a while." Lila is Pearl's cousin. Their family always helps us get ready for the gathering. Raymond, Edgar and a couple of the older boys are outside trying to hang canvas from the trees, just in case it should rain.

"All right, Pearl," I answer, returning my focus to the task at hand. The room is filled with humming, the slamming of cupboards and the clanging of utensils. Pearl is gathering the linens. Grandmother groans as she bends down to sift through the pots and pans.

I hear the back door open behind me and turn to see Posey standing in the doorway, hat in hands.

"Hi, Posey," I say.

"Hi," he responds, head down, his hands furiously twisting his hat.

"Posey," Pearl asks, "What you want?"

In mumbled speech, around a thick tongue, he replies, "I want to come inside."

"You done outside?" Pearl asks, moving toward him.

"Nah, Uncle Edgar got that ax out to chop them tree limbs. He told me to stay out of the way, to sit outside on the porch, but I don't like it there, it's lonely. I want to come inside with you, Aunt Pearl." I watch as Pearl warily glances in the direction of my grandmother.

"Posey," Pearl continues, "You do what your Uncle Edgar said. You go sit outside on the porch."

"Why?" he blurts.

"Cause you ain't supposed to be in the house." Posey doesn't move. His feet are planted firmly. Pearl and I cringe as he remains near the door, steadily rocking back and forth. Posey is a twenty-five year old black male. He was injured in a farming accident years ago which left a severe limp in his right leg and his right arm barely functional. In Pearl's words, "He took quite a lick. His brain is stuck at about seven or eight years old." Posey's emotions can change in a flash. Unfortunately, I was witness to one incident when Pearl had told him "no." He threw himself against a brick wall outside of the house, wailed wildly, and repeatedly beat his face with his own hands. By the time Raymond arrived to restrain him, Posey he had beaten his face to a pulp. It is in remembrance of that day that Pearl and I share a worrisome glance. Once again, Pearl turns to check the location of my grandmother.

"Posey, please go outside," Pearl pleads, standing over him.

"No."

"Please."

"No, I say . . . I want to stay . . .", but he doesn't finish. He extends his left hand beyond Pearl's waist. Pearl turns to see what he is reaching for and finds herself face-to-face with my grandmother who holds out a cookie. I watch as Pearl maneuvers for clearance.

"Posey," Grandmother says, softly. "Come here." Posey takes one step forward and strikes like a snake, grabbing the cookie. Oh, that was a mistake, I think to myself. "No!" grandmother says to him, slapping her hands against her thighs. "You do not eat that cookie until you are sitting down." Posey nods, holding the cookie securely in his hand. He focuses on grandmother's every move. "Now come over here," grandmother says, encouragingly, she points to a chair beside the stove. "Come on, Posey. You can sit here and enjoy your cookie."

Posey stands in place. Yes, I think, you had better take a minute. She is a worthy opponent. "No!" Posey yells. I drop my head against the table. "Posey," grandmother baits him, "If you move to the chair I will give you another cookie." I look up to see her standing near, her shoulders erect. Posey takes a moment to consider the offer before slowly, but surely, moving to the chair and perching himself on its edge. I believe I have just witnessed a miracle. "Good, now you just sit right here, Posey," grandmother says, in motion across the room. I relax and draw in a sigh of relief. "WOULD!" I about come out of my skin as she quickly turns around and continues, "you like a glass of milk, Posey?" she asks.

Who is this woman? I think. Posey gives her a toothless grin. "All right," she works her way over to the refrigerator and soon returns with a cold glass of milk. She sets the glass next to Posey on the stove. "You can stay in here, it's all right." she says.

"Yes'm, I can stay here. Right here!" Posey repeats, still smiling, cookie crumbs around his mouth, down his shirt and in his lap.

Pearl and I are speechless. You could knock us both over with a feather. We take a few seconds to collect ourselves before returning to our chores. Every few minutes I look over at Posey to find him deeply engulfed in a one-way conversation. He mumbles, "What's your name, Mister?" then answers himself, "My name is Posey!" he laughs a little. "Nice to meet you Posey!" he says with a wide grin. "Why it's nice to meet you too," he answers, laughing again. Oh, God, I think.

"Gal?" I hear my grandmother ask. Oh, God, I think again.

"Yes, ma'am?"

"You're probably finished. You can run on outside."

"Yes, ma'am." I begin to push my chair away from the table when I see that my grandmother is approaching me. Old instincts tell me to run, but I am cornered, still half under the table, my chair hooked in the rug. Helplessly, I look over at Pearl. She is already scurrying in my direction. I feel myself break a slight sweat as my grandmother, now beside me, raises her hand. I close my eyes. I feel her gently place her palm under my chin. "I'm sorry, Gal," she says, "I'm really sorry." I open my eyes in disbelief. What a strange day I've had, I tell myself. I remain still because she could still attack. From the corner of my eye, I see that Pearl is standing next to me like a guardian angel. My heart is beating loudly inside my chest. I say nothing. I can only hear Posey murmuring by the stove. I'm still alive, I think.

As I regain my composure, I hear a voice beside me say, "Go on. Say it." Pearl. I look up to see who she's speaking to. Me. She is nodding. I shake my head, no. She nods, yes. We have a code too.

Reluctantly, I mumble, "Me too," nearly choking on my tongue.

"Me too, what?" Pearls says.

"Me too, I'm sorry," I cut my eyes at her.

"Look at your grandmother and say it." I give Pearl my death-stare.

Slowly, I turn, moving my head toward my grandmother, my eyes still down. Unsure that even I believe what I'm about to say, "Sorry." Grandmother removes her hand from my chin and turns. She now stands toe-to-toe with Pearl. I plant my feet firmly on the floor, prepared to rise, need be. Pearl is standing straight, tall and undaunted.

"I have been horribly unkind to you, Pearl," Grandmother says. "I am terribly sorry. Do you think you can forgive this foolish old lady?"

"Yes'm," Pearl responds, "I believe I can."

Back at home, Pearl and I discuss the unlikely event. "Pearl," I insist, "Why'd you make me apologize to her? I didn't do anything to her."

"Well," she answers, "'Cause she's sorry. She's just trying to make things right," she solemnly faces me, "And you need to let her do that. In fact, you have to do that."

I am flabbergasted. "But . . ." I begin.

"This strictly calls for a yes or a no answer," Pearl leads, "So which is it?"

"It doesn't sound like you're giving me much choice," I huff. "Yes, yes, I'll try to do that."

"You can do it."

"But . . . if," I begin.

"No buts."

Chapter Twenty-Four

****

- *Address to the Nation* by President John F. Kennedy, Jr., October 22, 1962. President Kennedy informs the Nation of reports that on October 15, an American U-2 spy plane photographed nuclear missile sites being built by the Soviet Union in Cuba. The United States government has turned its focus to preparing the population for the possibility of nuclear attack.

****

My school days, fourteen to be exact, include that I and my classmates practice a technique aptly named the "duck and cover" method. At any point during the day the teacher might suddenly yell, "Drop" and we, the students, must automatically crouch under our desktops and take a protective stance by placing our hands behind our necks.

Now, I am no genius, but it seems obscure to me just how the placing of my hands behind my neck will somehow fend off a nuclear attack. I have little to no doubt that, if I am to survive, it will be thanks to the resolve and perseverance of my uncle, the survivalist.

Only minutes after the announcement of a possible attack, he sprang into action. He owns some wooded lots further out in the county, so it is simply a matter of building a fallout shelter. He, in a matter of days, completes a shelter large enough to hold our entire family. As it is with anything he endeavors, it is done in meticulous detail. The concrete walls are twelve inches thick and the shelter includes an air-handling and waste disposal system.

Shelter in place, he moves on to map out in painstaking detail, based on different scenarios, exactly how and where the family will gather to count heads and form a convoy to safety.

I am sad, aware that we very well may be the Earth's only remaining inhabitants. Yes, it will be lonely, but better than the alternative.

My uncle and I are deep in the woods. I am gathering twigs as instructed.

"Sammie Gal!" I hear my uncle yell. "Get over here."

I run to the edge of the shelter where he is standing deep in the crater. "What is it?" I look down.

"Just checking on you is all. How many sticks have you gathered?" he inquires.

"I've carried over about ten armfuls of twigs so far," I answer, awaiting further instructions.

"Okay, that's pretty good, but we're going to need a lot more. We got about forty people we need to provide for."

"Yes, sir, I'll keep gathering," and move to take a few steps back toward the woods.

"Oh," he yells loudly. "I just thought of something. You still out there?" He pops his head out the door. "I know how you are about that dog of yours, so I guess you plan to bring him with you?"

"Yes, sir." I begin to feel sick because he doesn't really like animals. He thinks they are, well, just animals.

"Okay, I'm going to say that's fine, but if you want him here "you" have to carry all his food and water. I am not carrying extra stuff just because you want that old dog. I'll get you here—you get your dog here. We clear on that? If "you" can't be bothered to make arrangements for him, then neither can I. We clear?"

"Yes, sir. Clear."

With a change in tone, he follows up, "Gal, you understand that we're going to be in this little shack for about two weeks?"

"Yes, sir, I know that."

"All right, remember to pack your good disposition." He smiles reassuringly and returns inside the shelter, carrying more jugs of water from the truck.

Then I think about Pearl and I run back a few steps. "Uncle," I yell.

"Huh," he steps back outside.

"What about Pearl?"

"Who?"

"Pearl, the lady who takes care of me."

"*Ahhhh*, Gal, don't do that to me. We were getting along so well."

"What?"

"Look, she's going to want to be with her family just like everybody else, and you got to be with yours. That's how it works. Only the strong survive. You understand that, don't you? If we bring her, then it'd be her son. Then her son would bring his wife, and on and on. We can't, Sam, sorry. Not open for discussion."

"Yes, sir," I answer returning to the woods.

Fortunately there was no nuclear attack, so we never have to actually use the shelter. Uncle continues to maintain the site, just in case, "You can't trust the damn government," he says, seriously. "First they take all your money, next they try to take away your guns. Pretty soon we won't have any rights at all," he forewarns. "The bastards," he adds out loud as an afterthought.

1963

***

- *CBS Evening News* with Walter Cronkite: June 10, 1963, of The Equal Pay Act which prohibits wage discrimination based on sex; in establishments where both men and women perform jobs that require equal skill, effort and responsibility.

***

- *CBS News Special Report*: June 11, 1963. We interrupt this regularly scheduled program for a special announcement by President John F. Kennedy. President Kennedy announces he will respond to the reports of the violence occurring at the University of Alabama by sending in 31,000 federal troops to restore order. Earlier in the day Governor George Wallace obstructed the entrance as two black students approached to enroll.

***

Our world is changing quickly. The outside violence is overwhelming. Residents hope it will not spill over into our small and relatively peaceful little town. I try to maintain a safe distance from the subject of race at home, and school, as there are too many varied opinions. I compare it to walking through a minefield. Defiance would be a fruitless waste of time, as I am inexperienced and still in a minority, young. More importantly, I am not willing to alienate myself from my family by debating an issue I will not win.

A few days prior to the scheduled "Great March on Washington" I am inside the five-and dime, my hand buried deep in jelly beans, when a black boy, who has helped out around there for years, approaches me. "Hey, Sam," he smiles, leaning against the candy counter.

"Hey, Sam, back," I respond in return. We were both about four years old when we discovered we have the same name, since then, that's how we greet each other.

"So, he asks, "What do you think about this March that's supposed to happen?"

"I only heard a little bit about it," I shrug, stuffing a handful of candy in my mouth.

"Well, I am pretty scared of it," he says. "Suppose some of those protesters come to town and start burning buildings and stuff. Dad said he's afraid the white residents here may think that the local blacks are causing the trouble and retaliate."

"Honestly, I don't know much about it." I am aware that my family serves as a sort of protective bubble for me. I've never known true fear. I have had some experience with the cause and effect of retaliation, but I know that I am sadly shallow and ill-uninformed on this topic. While I stand there feeling entirely inadequate, I also somehow feel compelled to offer him an alternative.

"Let's hope that doesn't happen, but if you are in danger, you can come to my house. I'll hide you upstairs in the attic. But, my Dad can't know. Don't take this wrong. He'd help you, but he won't, if he thinks he's putting his family in jeopardy by knowingly hiding you. So you'd have to come by yourself. You can't tell anybody what we've discussed. I will try to help you though if you need it. I can guarantee you one thing, if I can get you past Dad and upstairs into the attic, you'll be safe. No one will be coming through our front door, for sure."

"Thanks, Sammie," he says, "I really appreciate it." He and I give each other a shy wave and turn to leave. I walk to one side of town. He walks to the other.

—⚊w⚊—

"Pearl," I ask, leaning against the kitchen doorway, "I was talking to a friend earlier today. He said he is really worried about that March on D.C . . . Said he's afraid it may start trouble around here. How 'bout you, you afraid?"

"Lord, Child, where do you get these questions?" She sounds exasperated, but continues. "No, I ain't afraid. Uh-uh, no. Always some kind of price paid to move forward."

"Do you think there'll be trouble here in town?"

"No honey, not really, not here. D.C., maybe, but I don't live in D.C., so I ain't too worried." She *clicks* her way from the room, clearly avoiding any further conversation. I've known her long enough to understand that a quiet Pearl, is a worried Pearl.

****
- *NBC, The Huntley-Brinkley Report*: August 28, 1963, Dr. Martin Luther King, Jr., stands in front of the Lincoln Memorial where he delivers his message of hope to the approximately 250,000 people.

****

It is Wednesday, August 28. Pearl and I glance at each other as I move to turn on the television. She is settled on the couch. I pull the knob and return to a nearby chair.

As the television screen comes into focus, Pearl and I are shocked by the number of people that fill the Washington Mall. We watch as the camera man scans the crowd: the faces are not only blacks, but people from all races, ages, faiths and genders. We glance over at each another in disbelief.

I am very interested in the March, but really, I am more concerned about how it may affect Pearl and her family. As she watches the screen, I observe her.

"I say to you today, my friends," Dr. King says, "so even though we face the difficulties of today and tomorrow, I still have a dream." Pearl begins to rub her hands together, rather harshly, in a circular motion.

"I have a dream," Dr. King continues, "that my four children will one day live in a nation where they will not be judged by the color of their skin, but by the content of their character." Now I see the worry lines show prominently across Pearl's forehead. She looks over at me. I nod my support.

"And when we allow freedom to ring," he says. I am distracted as Pearl moves from her regular spot on the couch to the end nearer the television. I return my focus. "When we let it ring from every village and every hamlet," Dr. King continues, "from every state and every city, we will be able to speed up that day when all of God's children, black men and white men, Jews and Gentiles, Protestants and Catholics," Pearl perches her upper body over the arm of the couch and soaks in his every word. "We will be able to join hands and sing in the words of the old Negro spiritual: Free at last, free at last. Thank God almighty, we are free at last." The crowd roars, and Dr. King exits the podium. Pearl slides down from her perch. We are silent.

I understand that I cannot possibly know how she feels, so I decide that showing my support is the best option, "It will be okay, Pearl. It's good, time for change."

"Yes'm, I know it's time," she answers, uncommitted. I walk over to give her an encouraging hug, and exit the room. She needs some space.

****
- *CBS News Bulletin* with Walter Cronkite: November 22, 1963: "We interrupt this program for a special CBS News Bulletin with Walter Cronkite: (The television screen shows no visual other than the CBS logo.) "We are reporting a news bulletin from CBS News. In Dallas, Texas, three shots were fired at President Kennedy's motorcade in downtown Dallas. Our initial reports indicate that President Kennedy has been seriously wounded. We will remain on the air to report further details as they become available."

****

I am reading at my desk when the teacher distracts my attention. As I look up in her direction, she announces, "Boys and girls, the principal has requested that all students gather immediately in the school auditorium. Children, please line up, single file, by the door and remain quiet as you follow me into the auditorium. Once we arrive please quickly take a seat."

I am seated in the auditorium with several hundred others. It is unusually quiet. At about 2:30 p.m., I see the Principal walk on-stage. I note right away that this usually jovial man seems pained for some reason. He steps up to the microphone and clears his throat, before he announces, "Boys and girls. Earlier today nationwide television stations began reporting that President Kennedy had been shot in Dallas, Texas, his condition unknown. After a discussion with the Vice Principal, we agreed that there was no point in gathering all students in the auditorium until we had more information to give you. Then, just a few moments ago, it was confirmed that President

John F. Kennedy, Jr., died from his wounds. I am sorry. May he rest in peace." I watch as he clasps his hands and exits the stage.

My initial reaction is disbelief, after all, President Kennedy was simply too young to die. No one young, dies. He was handsome. Handsome people don't die, I rationalize. Someone has made a terrible mistake. I remain seated, buried deeply in my denial, hearing only the sobs and tears of my classmates resonating off the walls.

****
- *CBS Special Report* with Walter Cronkite: *CBS* has just received confirmation that President John F. Kennedy died today at 1:00 p.m. CST. At 2:38 aboard Air Force One, Lyndon B. Johnson was affirmed as President of the United States.

****
- *CBS News* with Walter Cronkite: September 15, 1963. We sadly report the death of four young black girls in a church in Birmingham, Alabama. The girls were attending a Sunday school class at the Sixteenth Street Baptist Church when a bomb exploded. Riots have erupted in response.

****

1964

Chapter Twenty-Six

****
- *The CBS News*, Monday, June 22, 1964, with Walter Cronkite: Today the bodies of three civil-rights workers from Ohio were located in Neshoba County, Mississippi. The last report on the whereabouts of the trio came in yesterday from the police, who said they were picked up for speeding on Sunday and released. Then late last night their burned-out station wagon was discovered near Bogue Chitto Swamp.

****
- *National Broadcast* from the White House, July 2, 1964. President Johnson reports to the Country as he prepares to sign The Civil Rights Act of 1964 in law. The Act will outlaw discrimination against blacks and women, and specifically the racial segregation of schools and the workplace or any facilities that serve the general public. Additionally, the Act calls for the creation of an Equal Employment Opportunity Commission.

****

My classmates and I have moved to middle school. Due to the location of the school, we'll have to ride a bus. It is also our first day of racial integration, which is causing some parents and grandparents, in particular, to feel extremely anxious.

Today my mother has chosen to drive me to school. She is justifiably apprehensive, as the local residents have varied and forceful opinions on the subject. She fears that some locals may over react.

"Okay, Sammie, I don't really expect any trouble, but around here you can never tell," Mother says, looking over at me.

"It will be fine, Mama. Don't make a big deal out of it."

"Yes, I know. I figure if there's going to be any trouble it will be outside at the parking lot entrance. So I will drive you there, and if it looks safe, let you out. You never can tell about some people around here, you know," she smiles over at me. We look back toward the house to see Pearl standing outside on the front porch, so mother gets out. "Pearl, what's the matter? Do you need me?" she yells.

"No, ma'am," Pearl answers, hands in her apron pockets.

"Well, just tell me, Pearl. Please, I've got to go." No response from Pearl so Mama gets back into the car. But Pearl is still standing there. "Geez," Mom says, getting out again. "Pearl, for God sake! What is it? Do you want to come with us?"

Immediately, Pearl shuffles down the steps toward the car. "Yes'm," she says, opening the car door. "That is, if you don't mind. I'd really like to see all those children going into the school together. Today is history, ma'am," she informs, now in the backseat of the car.

"That's fine, Pearl. I understand. I'll just bring you back before I go into work."

We stop in the school parking where I get out and turn to see Pearl with her face pressed against the window. There is no activity, other than the arrival of other parents dropping off their children, or the

"Yes'm"

arrival of school buses. Yet somehow, it feels different; the faces walking into the school are both black and white.

My mother turns to me, "It looks all right, Sam," she says. "You go on in, but if any trouble starts you just leave and go on home. I don't care if you get into trouble. Better safe, than sorry."

"Okay, Mom," I say, and step out of the car. Once outside, I bend over and motion for Pearl to roll down her window. I have to wait while she fumbles with it. The knob is missing. "Pearl, I'm going in now. You just sit right here and watch me."

"Yes'm, you just march yourself right on in there," she says.

Walking away, I hear Pearl whisper, "Lord, I never thought I would live to see this day."

I enter the school, scanning the area to get a lay of the land. There is a noticeable bustle in the air, but one I equate more with anticipation than apprehension. Across the entrance way, I see a list of homeroom assignments hanging on the wall. I am scanning for my name when I feel another student step up beside me. Since I have been in school with the same people since first grade, I automatically look up to see who it is, expecting to see a familiar face. Rather, I am looking straight into the faces of two black boys that I don't know. I feel something go through me, a slight twinge of discomfort. I try to process what it is I am feeling, and decide it's just a reaction to something new, that's all. Judging by the looks on their faces, they find my presence equally uncomfortable. I smile, and turn back to find my room number.

There are no racial incidents. Students go about their business, seeing it as just another boring school day. Occasionally, a black student will pass by me in the hallway, so we exchange a pleasant, low-keyed greeting. Everyone seems to recognize that we have to start somewhere, and may as well start today.

For the first few months, the white and black students do not interact very often. We simply don't have a lot in common. A mutual interest between the races is sports: basketball, baseball and football. The teamwork needed to be successful in these sports helps us get to know each other. Together, we cross the divide of ignorance. Most parents are encouraging and supportive, while most grandparents still struggle to adapt.

Outside of school, the older residents, black and white, keep to their usual routines, equal but separate. The barriers are beginning to fall. It is our time to lead.

1965

Chapter Twenty-Seven

****
- *ABC News Radio:* Today, March 7, 1965, will forever be remembered as "Bloody Sunday." Fifty marchers in Selma, Alabama, were hospitalized following the use of tear gas, whips and clubs against them by police. The group of protesters planned to walk to Montgomery, the state capitol, where they would present the Governor with a list of grievances. As they crossed the Edmund Perry Bridge toward their destination they were confronted and assaulted by state troopers.

****

Today, I passed and received my official Virginia State Driver's license. I took the test for the first time a few months ago, but failed because I couldn't parallel park. But today, at the ripe old age of fourteen years and nine months, I can legally drive, anywhere I want, alone.

"Saturday night! I love Saturday nights and there's a dance!" I yell to my mother, who's sitting in the next room. "I love my new dress, Mama. Thanks!"

"Oh, you can't have a good time in an old dress. Parties call for new dresses," she says, looking up as I enter the room. "Oh, Sammie, you look beautiful," a word rarely used to describe me. "Look," she says to my father, "Doesn't she look nice?"

"Of course," he answers, "She looks like you." I see Pearl peek around the corner from the kitchen, but she doesn't say a word. She lets me bask in my moment.

Recovered, I ask, "Mom, can I use your car?"

"Use your Daddy's."

"Why? His is ugly. No offense, Dad." I hear him scoff. "Mom, yours is little and cool. Please? I promise to stay where I'm supposed to and I won't wreck it."

"Oh, Sammie," she sighs, "All right, but you be careful in my car. You know I love that car."

"Thanks, Mom, you're wonderful."

"Yes, I am always wonderful. Especially when I do what you want."

"And is most of the time!" I step over to kiss her on the cheek.

I pull into the lot and search for a parking spot. I notice both blacks and whites are walking inside to the dance. That familiar twinge passes through my veins once again, another new situation to face. I am hoping things go perfectly tonight and everyone gets along.

Inside, the speakers are booming with Motown music, better known as "soul music." There are two groups gathered, each on opposite sides. The whites are on one side. The blacks are on the other. I remind myself that we are together at school every day, and that works out fine.

I enter through the glass doors and hear someone yell, "Sammie!" When I look around I see one of the black boys from my class.

"Yes'm"

He's walking my way, so I walk over to meet him somewhere in the middle.

"Isn't this great?" he says, excitedly.

"Yes, I just got here."

"You look great. I'd ask you to dance, but I don't think we're up to that yet," he laughs.

"Sorry, but I don't think I want to be the first to try that," I laugh, rather seriously.

"For sure," he nods. "I just wanted to say hi, Sammie. See you!" he says and returns to the other side of the room.

"Yes, see you," I say, but he is gone.

—∞—

I am dancing with one of the boys from class when a friend approaches. "Sammie, your Dad is here."

"Where?"

"Over by the door," she points in that direction. I walk over to the doors and see Dad standing just outside. He looks serious; his hands are in his pockets.

"Hi, Dad. What's up?"

"Nothing really, Sam. I just worry, and wanted to make sure that everything is going all right here."

I reach out and wrap my arms around his neck. "I didn't wreck Mom's car," I tease. "Dad, trust me. Don't worry. Really, everything is fine. Besides, my brave older brother is here to protect me."

He looks down and laughs. "Oh, I forgot that. Sammie, I didn't mean to embarrass you by coming here."

"No, Dad, it's all okay. You want to come inside? See Brother?"

Dad takes a small step forward, but decides against it. "No, another time," he says. He digs deep into his pocket and places four quarters in my hand. "If you need me, call. The pay phone is right there." He points to the booth behind me. "Give two quarters to your brother."

"Hey, Unc!" Patsy calls out as she passes by.

"Patsy!" he says, drawing her into a bear hug.

"Everything okay, here?" she asks, with an amused smile.

"Dad's just checking on me," I answer.

"Yeah, well, comes with the territory!" she laughs, returning to the dance.

"Dad, I promise to call if there's a problem. Otherwise, I'll see you shortly after midnight."

He steps up to kiss the top of my head. "I'll be waiting."

"Yes, I know."

The nights of music and dancing will soothe the soul of both savage beasts and hormonal teenagers. We make our greatest racial strides right here on the dance floor.

****

- *The Washington Star*: Today, July 2, 1965, one year after the passage of the Civil Rights Act of 1964, the Equal Employment Opportunity Commission is open. The Commission was founded to prohibit discrimination in employment on the basis of race, color, religion, sex or national origin.

****

1966

Chapter Twenty-Eight

***

- *The Washington Star Newspaper*: June 30, 1966. Today news was announced about the founding of a new organization, The National Organization of Woman (NOW). The group, led by author, Betty Friedan, stated the group is committed to bringing women into the mainstream of American society, exercising all privileges and responsibilities in equal partnership with men.

***

I am old enough to date. And, somehow, I have survived my awkward stage. Generally, I would be out with friends. But this particular evening, for some reason, I have chosen to stay home. I am sitting in the basement, watching television, when I hear my father bellow from upstairs, "Sammie! Get up here!"

I run upstairs, no dilly-dallying when Dad calls like that. "What?" I question as I come around the corner.

Standing by the front door, I see a local man, Mr. Pierce. He is dressed in a flannel shirt and coveralls, an unsavory sort, known to come from a family of like-minded unsavory sorts. He is glaring at me, possibly rabid. *I wonder why he's here?*

"Oh, Sam," Dad says, as I approach, "I wasn't sure you were here." Apprehensive, I sidle up next to my father, at the same time, keeping a wary eye on our guest.

When Dad turns to speak to Mr. Pierce I notice he sounds angry. "Is this the girl you saw?" he asks. "This is my daughter, Sammie."

Mr. Pierce takes a moment to examine me through his blood-shot eyes. I feel my skin crawl.

Finally, he answers, "No, it's the other one."

Frustrated, Dad attempts to clarify the answer, "What do you mean—the other one?"

"The other girl," Mr. Pierce says, "The one she's with all the time."

Confused, I ask, "Dad, can you tell me, what is . . . ." But I don't get to finish the question, as Dad interrupts, "Sam, wait. Just wait."

"Look," Dad says to Mr. Pierce, "What happens in my family is no concern of yours! I don't need you to keep me informed. Go on home now, and don't ever feel the urge to knock on my door again. Next time I may not be so welcoming." He slams the door in the man's face and stands back to look at me.

"Dad," I say, "Really? Just tell me what's going on." Outside, I hear Mr. Pierce preparing to leave, his car muffler just backfiring.

"He came here," Dad explains, "because he thought I ought to know something." Dad rolls his eyes. "He thought I should know that you were hanging out in a car full of black girls."

I have no idea how to respond to this claim: I could say, "So what?" or I could say, "That's none of his business;" or I could, and did, say "Dad, I was downstairs!"

I watch as my father walks over to his chair to sit down, head in hands. Worry obviously weighs heavy on his mind. "Sam, I know it wasn't you in that car, but do you have any idea who it may have been?" My mother stands off to the side of the room.

I stall, believing I know who it was in the car, but am hesitant to say. I run a quick mental summary: apparently, Mr. Pierce only knows that the girl he saw in the car is somehow related to my father. But, he doesn't know exactly how they are related. Must be her.

Dad waits impatiently for an answer. "Dad, I think I know who Mr. Pierce saw. But I don't want to say. Please, don't make me say. This is really silly. The 50s are over. It's not really important anymore."

"Sammie, without meaning to, you just answered me. There's only one person you would go to the grave for and that's Patsy. I won't ask you any more questions. You're absolutely right. It shouldn't be important, but I need to know in case I have to run interference against any other roughnecks out there like Mr. Pierce who may not agree with Patsy's particular choice of friends. Unfortunately, not everyone around here is, as you say, 'enlightened.'" I sit down on the hassock, facing my father.

"Dad, what's the big deal?" I ask. "I don't understand, what's wrong?"

"I can't believe I'm going to say this, Sam," Dad says, wringing his hands, "But here it is. It is one thing to be compassionate toward colored people; and quite another to be seen socializing with, dating, or especially, marrying a colored person. From where I sit, right now, those are two completely separate issues. They are choices that until today, I've never even had to consider. And, no matter how hard I try to remind myself that racism is wrong; no matter how much I struggle to accept what I know is right, I cannot. The fact is that I may never be able to accept it. I'm sorry, Sam." Dad looks up and holds his eyes on me to drive home his conviction.

While I don't agree with my father, I do appreciate his honesty. He admits that even he doesn't agree with his position. He admits it's something he's isn't proud of. But, I surmise, he has always been open-minded and adaptable. For now, in this particular moment, I decide to agree to disagree, nothing else. I hope he will someday overcome. I rise and turn to leave.

"Sam," Dad says, halting me. "Just one more thing," I remain still. "You keep your distance, but you also keep an eye out for Patsy. That man, and a thousand others just like him, could be dangerous. While I may not agree with Patsy's choice of friends, I do recognize that it's her choice to make it and that I will defend."

"Yes sir. I will." I say, about to move.

"One more thing," he adds. I stop. "I have absolutely no influence over how your grandfather might take it." I walk away.

Over the past couple of years, Patsy and I have moved into different circles of friends. She, being an athlete, extends her circle to include that group. I remain comfortably surrounded by my old friendships, those that began in elementary school. We rarely speak anymore. I occasionally consider counseling her about the possible consequences she may face, due to her choice of friends from our antiquated family. But, admittedly, I already know I will be less than persuasive as I try to push an agenda on her, that, I, myself, believe is out-dated, at best; and I seriously doubt she would heed my warning anyway. As the months come and go, I do a lot of soul searching and decide that, really, it isn't my decision to make. My job is just to love her, not question her rationale.

I do, however, dread a day when Patsy and I, due to our happenstance, may be faced with one of two choices: to either stand on the side of progress and enlightenment, possibly forfeiting our family; or stand within our family, such that it is, enlightened, but shackled. I will choose the latter. After all, I have been handling racial relations within my own household for years. I rationalize, that, just as Pearl predicted, progress is going to come, with or without me. But it won't come easily. And it will come much later for some than others—as both Patsy and I will come to learn.

****

- June 12, 1967, Supreme Court of the United States, *Loving vs. Virginia*: The Court declared Virginia's anti-miscegenation statute, the "Racial Integrity Act of 1924," unconstitutional, thereby ending all race-based legal restriction on marriage in the United States.

****

1968

*****

- *Address to the Nation* by President Lyndon B. Johnson: President Johnson recognizes the contributions and national mourning of civil rights leader, Dr. Martin Luther King. King was assassinated on April 4, 1968, at 6:01 p.m. as he stood on a balcony outside his hotel room in Memphis, Tennessee.

*****

- *US World & News Report*: Today, April 11, 1968, President Johnson signed the Civil Rights Act of 1968 into law. The bill prohibits discrimination in the sale, rental or financing of housing based on race, religion, national origin, sex, handicap or family status.

*****

It's Easter and the family is gathered together at the old house, just like old times. I am standing in the living room wrapped in nostalgia as I survey the men once again gathered in the living room without the one-time cloud of smoke. I can hear the women gathered in the kitchen, their laughter carrying down the hallway. My heart carries me back through many years in this place. I am at home, and at peace. The third generation, mine, is largely grown. A few of my cousins are now attending college. They will be back today for dinner. Brother is married and his wife is expecting their first child any day.

As I stand lost in time, I hear the crunch of gravel in the driveway and walk over to the glass door to look outside. My heart is full as her car pulls into the driveway. "Hey," I yell to the others, "She's here!" and move closer to the door. I cannot wait to wrap her in my arms. But I am the only one who appears to be excited. I note that mine is the only ecstatic voice in the room. I turn to look behind me. The men have all risen from their chairs and stand grimly in place. Their faces are drawn and solemn. The expression on their faces, alone, carries me back in time to the racial ugliness of the 1950s and early 1960s. I feel a familiar twinge of dread. I know that, yet again, I have been left outside the loop.

It is my grandfather who moves forward, slower perhaps, but I still recognize his posture of self-righteous determination. I step aside to let him pass.

"Mama?" I turn and say. She walks up beside me and wraps her arm around my shoulders. "Sammie, I don't agree with this. I want you to know that," she says, lovingly.

"With what? Just what the hell is going on here?" The next few minutes rush forward, carrying me with them like a river.

Patsy cracks open the front door and steps inside. She is greeted by the bigotries of our past. I stand. Mute.

I hear the words resonate, "You are no longer welcome here," as if I were standing on the other side of a partition. I seek out the source of cruelty and cannot believe those words were uttered by our kind and dedicated grandfather. I watch as Patsy's eyes sweep helplessly through the room, I know, for me. For an instant our eyes meet. I drop mine to the floor, unsure and weak.

As I lift my eyes, I see her wide smile is gone. Her chin is quivering, her nose taking on a red hue and the tears that flood her aqua eyes make their way down her face. Her desperation robs me of caution, so I step forward. "What is wrong with everyone? What do you think you're doing? You can't do this! You can't just pretend to love someone one day and suddenly not. Either you do or you don't." My words are part reprimand, part begging for mercy.

"By God", grandfather turns to me, "About a week ago one of the neighbors came here to tell me that she was dating a colored boy! A colored boy! I didn't believe it! I told him to get off my property! But then, a few days ago, I decided to go see for myself. I drove over to the school and parked out back. I sat there a while when, sure enough, the two of them came out of that school, walking hand-in-hand. Hand-in-hand!" I watch as he lowers his head and places his worn old hand over his heart for a moment. "She," he soon continues, "has brought disgrace upon our entire family!" He now steps closer to me. His body language speaks volumes. I am horrified, but not afraid.

I draw in a deep breath, prepared to protest, when I feel the weight of my father's hand rest on my shoulder, a subtle warning that anymore from me on this matter may bring consequences I don't want. Grandfather, seeing that I have been suppressed, returns his focus to Patsy.

From behind me I hear my mother's voice, "Sammie, come here baby." It seems she is miles away. My feet are heavy and I remain motionless. My much anticipated happy day has turned out to be one of the most shameful and gut-wrenching days of my fairly short life. My heart is broken. Soon, mother is at my side. My father is walking away, across the room, in search of a neutral position. His face shows his inner struggle.

"Do not come here again!" my Grandfather growls. "We do not know you!" he yells, reaching deep into his pocket for a hankie to wipe the tears from his face. I watch as he shuffles closer to Patsy. They are now standing toe-to-toe, both crying. No words.

Again, Patsy looks across the room at me. She struggles to recover her resolve, holding her head high and arching her shoulders back. "Sammie, don't you cry," she comforts, "I will be fine. I am more worried about leaving you here." My head crushes to my chest as I think, *Yes, me too*. Patsy wipes the tears from her face and focuses individually on her one-time loving family. Finished, she turns to leave. And I will never see her in the old place again.

****

- *Mutual Broadcasting System*: Shortly after midnight, today, June 5, 1968, as Robert "Bobby" F. Kennedy exited, just moments after his victory in the California Democratic primary, in Los Angeles, was shot. Our reporter, Andrew West, was at the event and captured the shooting on tape. Senator Kennedy was rushed to The Good Samaritan Hospital where, we understand, he is currently undergoing surgery. We will keep you up to date as additional news arrives.

****

Following the holiday fiasco I am quick to approach my father. "Dad, please tell me you don't agree with that decision?"

"Well, it isn't up to me Sammie. My options are not good. That is my father, after all, and I cannot turn my back on him. He's too old to overcome the prejudices of his era. Would you turn your back on me because I said or did something foolish in my old age?"

"No, sir," I reply, "never." I immediately get his point and, reluctantly, relent.

"I am sure, Sam, that Patsy was well aware of the consequences she might face when she made her decision," he continues. "It was not my decision, nor yours, to make. She made it. Hopefully, she can live with it."

Distraught, I retreat to my bedroom.

****

- *BBC Special Announcement*: June 6, 1968. Senator Kennedy's Press Secretary, Frank Mankiewicz, stepped up to a podium at *Good Samaritan Hospital,* "Senator Robert Francis Kennedy died at 1:44 today."

****

Monday morning, bright and early, Pearl arrives. I can hear her humming as the key turns in the lock. I hear her shuffling feet headed toward my room. I pull the pillow over my head. Soon the doorknob turns and a precious Pearl enters.

"Good morning child! Time to get up! I trust you had a nice Easter!"

From underneath the pillow, I answer, "It was just horrible, Pearl."

"Lord, child, what in the world." She shuffles quickly to the bed, sits down and pulls the pillow off my head. She works to position what she can of my now adult body into her lap. "Tell Pearl," she says. "Tell me."

"I can't, Pearl. It was just too embarrassing to even repeat."

"Honey, Pearl been embarrassed before. Now tell me. You'll feel better. We'll figure this thing out just like we always does." She strokes my hair.

Suddenly, I have been transported to my safest place. I am once again four years old, locked safely in her arms. I await her words that will help me survive.

It takes a long time for me to tell the story. Pearl never says a word. She listens and hums occasionally. Finally, I reach the ending. "Pearl, Granddad was so mean. I barely recognized him yesterday."

"Well, baby, let me say this, he ain't mean. The world is changing pretty fast for your Granddad. Times are spinning out of his control, and that's a new thing for him. Oh, he always have control before, but now, see, he don't. He was the smartest one. Now he's not. What he said went. Now no one's listening. Worse, someone challenged him in front of the others, and he's just doing what he thinks his Daddy would have done. He can't change, much less admit that he wishes he could. He's caught up in a whirlwind with no way out. Least that's what Pearl thinks."

"He was mean, Pearl," I insist.

"Nah, honey, he ain't. He ain't the 'down to the bone' kind of mean. He's been good to my family. He's just being stubborn and prideful. Know what they say? 'Pride goes before the fall.'" She looks at me and continues, "He be falling, baby, and you shouldn't abandon him. "Your Granddaddy, he may come around, just give him some time."

"I really hope so, Pearl," I answer, still resting in her arms.

"Forgiveness is a powerful thing. I hope you can try to forgive him, child, otherwise, you'll be looking for answers to something that ain't never going to come. Why this? Well, 'cause. Why that? Well, 'cause. That's what Pearl thinks anyway." She nods.

"Oh, Pearl, why do you do that?"

"Now what'd I do?"

"You always know what to say."

"Cause . . . . I'm smart," she smiles. "Now get your sorry self out of that bed right this minute. Then go see your Grandpa. I think he needs you."

Over the years, Patsy and I stay in touch—on the sly we call it—but our bond of old is gone and dwindles more with each passing year. Our childhood bond is cut down like unwanted weeds. Pearl would try to comfort me. "All we can do is pray, that someday, Mister's heart will soften and allow Patsy back into his life."

But I will never hear him speak her name again; nor may it be spoken in his presence. I am not sure if his stance is driven by pure stubbornness, age or, possibly, a broken heart. But, we all lost.

On Easter Day, several years later, Patsy will die. And so will a piece of myself.

1969

Chapter Thirty

****

- *CBS Evening News* with Walter Cronkite: Today, November 15, approximately two million Americans, across the nation, took part in The Peace Moratorium; it is believed to have been the largest demonstration in United States history. The movement was in protest to a continuation of the war in Vietnam. In Washington, D.C., the crowd was estimated at 250,000 people.

****

The phone rings and I ask Pearl to answer it. A few seconds later, I hear her say, "Okay, yes sir, I'll tell her. Mister, don't you do nothing, you hear me? I'm going to get her right now. You just wait there." Then I hear the phone hit its cradle and the shuffling of familiar feet headed in my direction.

"Miss Sammie, Miss Sammie!" Pearl yells frantically. "Oh Lord, girl you need to get to your Granddaddy's house lickety-split. He done something! I know it! He said the police are there. He said for me to tell you to come over to the house right now!" She is circling in the hallway, hands on her head.

"Pearl," I say, "calm down. I'm going to go. You better call Daddy."

"Oh, no, I can't do that. Don't make me do that. Mister told me, plain, not to tell anyone but you." She hands me my wallet. "You better go!"

"I am going, but you need to calm down. I'm sure it's nothing." I stand nearby as she shakes out her arms and draws in a few deep breaths. "Pearl, you're just slowing me down."

"Yes'm. I'm all right, you go on now," and shoos me away with her hands. "Go, Child!"

With that I leave the house. I am well aware that I am walking into a situation where my father has been purposefully circumvented. Indeed, I am right. As I near the house I can see police cars parked in the driveway so I start running. Grandfather is standing outside on the porch, waiting for me.

"What happened?" I call out as I get near.

"I think I'm in a lot of trouble, Gal," he mumbles. "You know those little bastards, the ones that keep running across my yard. The ones I told to keep off my property. Well . . . . ," his eyes glance over my right shoulder as a policeman finishes for him, "Your grandfather shot buckshot at two kids who were walking through his yard."

Sadly I can understand my grandfather's frustration, so I laugh. "Granddad, you can't just go around shooting at people."

"Well, Gal, they were on my property. It's my property and I have the right to defend it. That's a man's God-given right, last I know." He nods firmly at the officer to drive his point home.

I shrug, not knowing quite how to answer that. I think he does have a point, at least according to the laws he grew up with. "Officer," I turn, fighting off a smile, "If I take his shotgun away and he promises not to shoot at the little bastards anymore, will you let it go?"

Apparently entertained, he answers, "Yes, ma'am, this time."

"Well, you better just hold it right there," Granddad interrupts, looking at the officer. "What you going to do about those little bastards?"

"I'm going to tell them they better stay out of your yard because they might get shot," he smirks.

With that, Granddad lodges his hands deep into his pockets, fiddles with his change. "And you be sure to tell them had I meant to hit them, I would have."

"Yes, sir, I surely will."

I wait until the cruisers pull away and carry the shotgun back inside.

"Granddad, you made me lie to that officer because I am not going to take your shotgun," I say, "but you can't be shooting at anybody, you hear me? You call the police or Daddy if you're concerned about something. I'd hate to see you spend the rest of your life in jail somewhere." I bend to return the shotgun to its rightful place in the pantry.

He's standing still, looking at me. "You going to tell?"

"Are you kidding? Of course, I'm not telling! And if you tell I'm going to deny it! I don't know anything!" I look over and he is smiling. "Look," I continue, "It's our little secret, but if you do something dangerous like this again I'm going to have to tell. And if Dad finds out I know about this, he's going to have both our hides. Promise me. You won't use that shotgun?" I head toward the door and remember I promised to call Pearl. "I have got to call Pearl," I say.

"Why?"

"Oh, I think since she's the one who answered the phone and told me to come here . . ." He nods in agreement.

I dial the house and Pearl answers. "Child? What that old fool gone and done now?"

"Pearl, I'll explain when I get home. I'm on the way. Don't tell anybody. Okay?"

"If there's one thing you should know by now, it's that Pearl can keep a secret," she scoffs.

Once again, I make my way to the front porch. As I pass by my grandfather, he gives me a firm pat on the back and says, "Okay, Gal. I thank you so much for dropping by. Come see me again," as if we were wrapping up a pleasant visit.

"Welcome," I say, and jump over the front steps. I am headed for home.

—⁂—

A few weeks later, as Granddad sits at his kitchen table, a stranger walks right through his unlocked door and grabs the car keys from a hallway hook. He is perplexed by the boldness of the intruder, and watches as the man clears the porch steps and walks to the car. The burglar obviously has a false sense of security, considering the age of his victim, but he is neither clever, nor quick enough to outsmart decades of experience. Before he gets to the garage, Granddad retrieves "old faithful" from the pantry and steps out onto the porch. Gun in hand, he yells, "I think you better hold it right there, young fella!" *Click.*

The police report reads that the perpetrator was found restrained at gunpoint upon their arrival.

It is my father who confiscates the shotgun for good.

—⚬—

Several months later, Granddad is stopped by the police for speeding and going the wrong way down an interstate highway. Dad, as the eldest, is the one who makes the decision to take his car keys. It is an ugly day.

"Come on, Gal," Dad says to me as I recline comfortably on the couch. Pearl is dusting the living room furniture nearby.

"Why do I have to go? He is not going to like this one little bit. He is going to be so mad and I don't want him mad at me. He is going to cuss you so bad." Pearl continues to dust the furniture, flitting from here to there.

"Yes, I suspect he will." Dad answers, "That's why you're going. He's partial to you. Maybe you can help me calm him down."

I climb off the couch to follow my father outside, but as I reach back to close the door I hear a faint and familiar, *"Um, um, um, poor old Mister. Um, um, um."*

—⚬—

We arrive at the house and go inside. I sit quietly in the corner, hoping to become invisible.

Granddad is puffed up like a Siamese cat. "Who the hell are you to be taking my car keys? Who the hell died and left you in charge?" he questions his son.

"Dad, I'm taking them because I love you, and I don't want you to hurt anyone." By this time my uncle has entered the room and stands off to the side, listening to the conversation. Grandfather turns to look at him. "I would suggest you not put your car keys down—this one here might take them. He's got a key thing or something," and turns to leave the room. My uncle smiles and heads outside to disable the car—that is his job.

Due to the recent antics of my Grandfather, it is becoming apparent that he is not only a danger to himself, but others as well. A family meeting is called and, rather than meet at the old house, they all gather at ours. The bottom line is that he needs a caretaker. Grandmother passed away three years ago and there has been a decline in him since, physically and emotionally.

It is my father, his brothers and sister who discuss the options. But it is Pearl who comes up with the answer.

"Sir," Pearl interrupts, "I don't want to get in your family business or anything, but we both know that Miss Sammie don't really need me anymore. You just keeping me on because you know I need the job, but really, you're just giving me the money. We both know that." She stands, focused on him.

No reply from my father. He leans forward, resting his elbow on his knees. She has just called his bluff.

She continues, "I been thinking that since you all need somebody to help with Mister, and since I have known him a long time, that I might be the best one to take care of him. He was mighty good to my parents and I know they would want me to help him. It'd be just fine with me. You know I love this family like I love my own, but I really want to do it."

Dad looks at her hesitantly. "Pearl, that's very nice of you, but he's bull-headed and awfully hard to get along with. Lord only knows what will come out of his mouth. I don't want him to hurt your feelings. So I just can't put you in that position."

"Ain't nothing he can say, that I ain't heard before. I know he don't mean it. You just let me worry about those things. There ain't nobody left around here who knows him better than I do. If it gets too hard, I'll just tell you." She tips her head.

"Pearl," Dad answers, "You've been with me most of my life . . . I . . . ," his voice drifts away.

Mother steps into the conversation. "Okay, Pearl. If that's what you want to do, I suggest we try it for a few days, just to see how it works. You can always change your mind. I will pick you up just the same as always and take you home."

"Yes'm," Pearl answers.

—◊—

Dad and I decide to wait about two weeks before we return to the old house. Our hope is that Pearl will settle in and take charge, which is no easy feat. As we get near, Dad and I hear Granddad's yelling voice somewhere in the living room.

"Pearl, where is my lunch? It's noon. I always eat right at noon!" We climb the steps and crack the front door.

Pearl's familiar voice answers from the kitchen, "It ain't noon yet, Mister. Its five minutes till. Just hold your horses!"

We peer in and expect to see his angry face, but his eyes shine with mischief. "That Pearl," he says, "She's a pistol. Kind of bossy though."

We wait while Pearl, carries in a tray that she hands to him and he, in turn, balances on his knees.

"Well, you sure took your sweet time about it!" he says, looking up at her.

"Mister, why are you trying my patience?" She stands over him. "Lord knows that Pearl has tons of patience. *Um, um.*" She looks up at the sky and asks, "Lord, why you so mad at me?"

****
- *CBS Live Broadcast* with Roger Mudd: Today, December 1, 1969, citizens held their breath as the Selective Service National headquarters placed 366 blue plastic capsules into a large container, followed by an indiscriminate drawing. Each capsule contained within it a birth date to be used as the "order of call" for all men, born between 1944 and 1950, to serve in the Vietnam conflict.

****

Within the year, time will claim my grandfather, still harboring his stubbornness. Pearl is now weak and in declining health herself. She has worked since she was a young girl, steadily, faithfully and fearlessly. Dad and mother ask her to return to work for us. She has agreed. She and I are sitting outside on the old familiar swing. I rock while she snaps beans into a pot on her lap.

"Pearl?" I ask.

"Yes, child?" She turns to look at me. I note that her eyes look especially tired.

"How are you doing? I watch as her back stiffens and she stares into my eyes.

"You know, I think that's the first time you've ever asked how I been doing?"

"Is it? I'm sorry, Pearl. I guess I thought all you had to do was take care of me." I cock my head teasingly and push off on the porch.

"Oh, don't get me wrong. I'm really lucky. You, your Mama and Daddy care about me—else I wouldn't be working here and getting paid to snap these silly beans," she laughs. "Just feels kind of funny to know the people you're supposed to be taking care of are actually taking care of you, only no one wants to admit it. Pride sure is a funny thing. *Ummm . . . ummm."*

"Hey Pearl? How many scoldings do you think you gave me in this swing?"

"A lot, I guess, but not nearly enough!"

****
- *CBS News* with Walter Cronkite: Today, July 20, 1969, we bring you live coverage of the Apollo 11 Moon landing from Cape Canaveral, Florida.

****

Chapter Thirty-One

There's an early morning knock at the front door. Because it's such an unusual hour for visitors, the entire family heads in that direction.

Mom reaches the door first. Standing outside on the porch, hands in pockets, is Raymond, Pearl's brother. His smile is missing.

"Hi, Raymond," Dad says, greeting him. "Come on in. You're up a might early? Want some coffee?"

"No, sir. I mean, Mister. I mean Mister Richard, Sir." He fumbles a few seconds, "I'm sorry, I just can't get used to calling you Richard. Can I just call you Mister? Feels better." Dad smiles and nods. "I came to let you know that this morning Sister Pearl suffered a massive stroke. Right now, things don't look too good for her."

"Oh, my God!" My mother cries, reaching for a *Kleenex*.

"Come on, Dad! We have to go to her!" I say. "We can take her to the hospital or call Doc Luther to come look at her."

"Miss Sammie," Raymond interrupts, "Pearl told me that she does not want to go to the hospital. I asked. I called a doctor, who did come to check her. He offered to send her to the hospital, but she said she is just very tired, and would like to stay home with her family. We are going to do what she wants."

"No . . ." I begin.

"Let it go, Sam," Dad says. "We have to be respectful of Pearl's wishes. That's what she would want from us. And it's what she deserves. It's not about what we want. It's all about Pearl, honey. Raymond," he continues, "What can we do to help?"

A few days later, on a beautiful spring day, Raymond stops by the house to let us know that Pearl has died. Right now I am sitting on the couch, thinking about all the days we have shared, the trials and triumphs. The days I spent in that lap, the *clicking*, the humming and the lessons. How much I am going to miss her.

I recall her plea, "You grow up to be a good girl. Don't ever be mean to nobody just 'cause of their color or what they have and don't have. You love and care for your Mama and Daddy. Handle each day one at a time and give it all you have to give." With all those memories, I move to Pearl's favorite sitting cushion and cry out my loss, as best I can.

A memorial has been scheduled at the local Baptist Church, just beyond the tracks. Dad said the gathered mourners will probably consist of her family and long-time friends from church. I have asked if we could go, but Dad believes our presence there might be a distraction. "It's Pearl's day," he says, "We don't want to take anything away from her. God knows, she deserves all the attention."

It's the day of the funeral and I am walking through town. I have reached the railroad tracks and am crossing over near the old elementary school. My destination is a hill behind the feed store.

I am hopeful that the top of that hill might be the perfect position where I can sit and watch the funeral, but not be seen as a distraction. I finally reach the store, jump a narrow creek, and sullenly climb the hill. At the top I hunker down underneath an old maple tree, it's cooler than normal, so I wrap my sweater tightly around me.

Soon the hearse and cars begin to pull into the graveyard, so I slump down a little closer to the ground. While the minister takes his position I can see Lila and Posey, Raymond and Edgar as they move toward a front row of chairs. Posey, with his special intuition, spots me. He waves innocently. In response, I raise my hand and ripple my fingers. He sits.

I am so engrossed in sorrow that I do not hear anyone approach from behind. I look up to see him, hat in hands. "Great minds, huh?" Yes, I nod. He lowers himself down beside me, takes my hand, and, together, we share our final good-byes to Pearl. We can't hear the sermon, but it doesn't really matter. We are here, together, like she'd want.

"That one little black woman sure left a mark," he says. I nod.

"I love you, Dad," I say.

"Me too," he responds.

I would like to thank my hometown friends, particularly Sharon Gregory Jacobs, E. Thomas Fife and Bobbie Latimer Cloud, for their encouragement and support on this project. New friends are nice, but old friends are simply irreplaceable.

I must thank my biggest supporter, my husband, who has tirelessly listened to my vamps and revamps of memories so completely foreign to him that it is impossible for him to relate. I am sure he felt as though he had crossed a time warp as he took his place among my numerous family seniors, but undaunted, he held many wrinkled hands, distributed thousands of comforting hugs and remained a steadfast guardian as each departed from our lives.

To my brother, you will always be my hero. Thanks for your support and encouragement, on my book, and in my life.

To my children, I pray that you carry on with the same fortitude and determination that runs through your veins. Not every day is easy, nor everything perfect; but represent, take your place, set your expectations, and then own them. Be mindful that you will certainly have regrets, but regrets are as much a part of a full life as your successes. Remember that time will demand you adapt. Today, you are in the zone; tomorrow, you will be out of touch. Prepare yourself, it's difficult, trust me.

To my readers, "Thank you, so much!" I really hope you enjoyed reading "Yes'm". I enjoyed writing it!

Please Allow Me Liberties in the Following Areas

POST-TRAUMATIC STRESS SYNDROME

I am not a physician, but a brief research leads me to believe that Post Traumatic Stress Disorder (PTSD) was not an official diagnosis until 1980. I would suspect, prior to that, the nearest and most popular term used to describe a suffering veteran, particularly a World War II veteran, was, perhaps, "shell shock" or "battle fatigue." But I recall those terms being used so vaguely, to describe so many veteran issues, that they were given little merit by the general public.

JIM CROW LAWS

The Jim Crow laws referenced in the book are substantially abbreviated, but taken from actual legislation that existed, intermittently, across the South.

J. M. Duke

BROADCASTERS/JOURNALISTS DISCLOSURE

I have conducted rather extensive research in an attempt to accurately represent the news broadcasters, journalists and stations relevant to the issues raised in my timeline reports. However, for story-telling purposes, where unable to confirm an actual report or reporter, I have attached the names of broadcasters relevant to the time and era, who may or may not have been involved.

References

BOOKS:

Brinkley, Douglas. *Cronkite*. New York: HarperCollins Publishers. 2012. Print.

Boyd, Herb, and Todd Burroughs. *Civil Rights: Yesterday & Today*. West Side Publishing, 2010. Print

ELECTRONIC SOURCES:

Shedden, David, April 4, 2006, Sep. 8, 2011, Early TV Anchors/Poynter, http://www.poynter.org/uncategorized/74607/early-tv-anchors September 6, 2012

Leonard Miall. August 18, 1995, Obituaries: John Cameron Swayze—People—News—The Independent, Sept. 11, 2012. http://www.independent.co.uk/news/people/obituaries-john-cameron-swayze-1596728.html

Archival Television Audio: Civil Rights Samper, Nov. 1, 1956 (Douglas Edwards and the News), http://www.audioandtext.com/ATA/transcripts/ATA_Sampler1_1960_01_01_1_Transcript.html September 6, 2012.

Asheboro Rotary Club—Asheboro, North Carolina, District 7690, *The Tar Wheel*, January 23,2009, http://www.ashebororotary.com/archives/2009/TarWheel_2009_01_23.pdf
September 11, 2012.

Greensboro, North Carolina—Fun Facts, Questions, Answers, Information, http://funtrivia.com/en/subtopics/Greensboro-North_Carolina-298162.html
September 6, 2012.

WGBH Education Foundation, 1996-2010, WGBH American Experience Freedom Riders People Howard K. Smith CBS/PBS, http://www.pbs.org/wgbh/americanexperience/freedomriders/people/howard-k-smith-cbs
September 6, 2012.

John F. Kennedy Presidential Library and Museum, Cuban Missile Crisis—John F. Kennedy Presidential Library & Museum, http://www.jfklibrary.org/JFK/JFK-in-History/Cuban-Missile-Crisis.aspx
September 9, 2012.

John F. Kennedy Presidential Library And Museum, Report to the American People on Civil Rights, 11 June 1963, http://www.jfklibrary.org/Asset-Viewer/LH8F_0Mzv0e6Ro1yEm74Ng.aspx
September 6, 2012.

Wikipedia.com, CBS Evening News—Wikipedia, the free encyclopedia, Walter Cronkite(1962-1981)
http://en.wikipedia.org/wiki/CBS_Evening_News
September 6, 2012.

History.com, JFK faces down defiant governor—History.com This Day in History—6/11/1963, http://www.history.com/this-day-in-history/jfk-faces-down-defiant-governor September 8, 2012.

Public Papers of the Presidents of the United States: Lyndon B. Johnson 1963-64. Volume II, entry 336, pp.842-844. Washington, D.C. Government Printing Office, 1965, President Lyndon B. Johnson's Radio and Television Remarks Upon Signing the Civil Rights Bill, http://www.lbjlib.utexas.edu/johnson/archives.hom/speeches.hom/640702.asp September 8, 2012.

Collector's Choice Audio—Civil Rights Movement (1956—1968), Archival Television Audio—Civil Rights Movement (1956-1968), http://www.atvaudio.com/ata_civilrights.php. September 6, 2012.

EEOC.gov., 1965-1971: A "Toothless Tiger" Helps Shape the Law and Educate the Public, http://www.eeoc.gov/eeoc/history/35th/1965-71/index.htm September 8, 2012.

Devon-Ritchie, August 7, 2012, The Washington Star Closes, Ending 128 Years of Operation. http://famousdaily.com/history/washington-star-closes.html. September 25, 2012

About.com. Women's History. National Organization for Woman—NOW. http://womenshistory.about.com/od/feminism/p/now.htm September 25, 2012

CBS News.com, 1968 King Assassination Report (CBS News)—Youtube, April 3, 2008, 1968 King Assassination Report (CBS News)
http://www.youtube.com/watch?v=cmOBbxgxKvo
September 8, 2012.

Examiner.Com, Patricia Hysell, Civil Rights Act of 1968—National this day in history/Examiner.com, April 11, 2010.
http://www.examiner.com/article/civil-rights-act-of-1968
September 8, 2012.
Youtube.com, Robert F. Kennedy death announcement, http://www.youtube.com/watch?v=ujPidSx7Vus
September 9, 2012.

DavidVonPein2, January 9, 2010, Robert F. Kennedy is Assassinated (Andrew West's Radio Coverage)
http://www.historynet.com/live-from-dc-its-lottery-night-1969.htm
September 12, 2012.

U.S. Equal Employment Opportunity Commission, The Equal Pay Act of 1963 (EPA)
http://www.eeoc.gov/laws/statutes/epa.cfm
September 25, 2012

PBS.org. The Sixties War & Peace/PBS, http://www.pbs.org/opb/thesixties/topics/war/index.html.
September 6, 2012.

Search Wikipedia, Loving v. Virginia, Supreme Court of the United States, http://www.en.m.wikipedia.org/wiki/Loving_v._Virginia.
September 10, 2012.

CPSIA information can be obtained at www.ICGtesting.com
Printed in the USA
BVOW080912021112

304492BV00001B/2/P